IRON MAN, IRON HORSE

IRON MAN, IRON HORSE

Will Cook

Chivers Press • G.K. Hall & Co.
Bath, England   Thorndike, Maine USA

This Large Print edition is published by Chivers Press, England, and by G.K. Hall & Co., USA.

Published in 2000 in the U.K. by arrangement with the author c/o Golden West Literary Agency.

Published in 2000 in the U.S. by arrangement with Golden West Literary Agency.

U.K. Hardcover ISBN 0-7540-4303-7 (Chivers Large Print)
U.K. Softcover   ISBN 0-7540-4304-5 (Camden Large Print)
U.S. Softcover   ISBN 0-7838-9176-8 (Nightingale Series Edition)

The text of this Large Print edition is unabridged.
Other aspects of the book may vary from the original edition.

Set in 16 pt. New Times Roman.

Printed in Great Britain on acid-free paper.

British Library Cataloguing in Publication Data available

Library of Congress Cataloging-in-Publication Data

    Cook, Will.
    Iron man, iron horse / Will Cook.
        p. cm.
      ISBN 0-7838-9176-8 (lg. print : sc : alk. paper)
      1. Railroads—Fiction. 2. Large type books. I. Title.
    PS3553.O5547 I75 2000
    813'.54—dc21

                                       00–057535

CHAPTER ONE

Ben Holliday always started his day with a careful shave because he was a methodical man even in the smallest details of his day-to-day living. When the seven o'clock roundhouse whistle called the men to work, he was either wiping the blade of his razor or putting it in its case. Holliday was an angular man, nearly six feet tall, and a bit on the slender side, but a month of this dry summer air of North Texas had so improved his appetite that he expected this condition to change, and after each shave he examined his cheeks to see if there was any increase in fullness there. His face, at thirty-two, was beginning to show more of what he was; his manner of thinking was casting permanent lines on his forehead, pulling his rather thin lips into continually sterner lines until the general impression he gave upon first glance was that here was a man who did not laugh enough.

Holliday was a man seemingly overcome by his desire to do well.

Perhaps it was this honesty, this ambition, that made him a little bitter every time he walked a few steps from his quarters to his office and saw the name on the frosted glass of the door. It had a pomposity, a touch of sham, like a man who went around and bragged about his horse which was dying.

BENJAMIN C. HOLLIDAY
CHAIRMAN OF THE BOARD
MIDLAND-PACIFIC RAILROAD

He liked the office because it gave him an uninterrupted, second-story view of the empty cattle pens, and the idle switchyard, and the roundhouse, which was rapidly running out of work to do. He could also see the miles of track running south through the dry valley where the wind blew the weeds growing between the ties and rolled tumbleweeds and piled dust in windrows against the rails, now dull red with rust. Holliday felt that he should look at that every day, to remind him of what he had to do, to remind him that two men from before him had failed. One hundred and eighty miles of railroad going broke, and it was his job, his sole function, to get the rust off those rails.

It had been nearly six months since a train had gone south; his only knowledge of the country was what he could see from his window, the miles stretched out flat and lonely and baked under a constant sun. It was Indian country, and cattle country, with the only civilized mark upon it being the railroad tracks arcing out toward a blue haze-veiled rim of mountains nestled low against a far horizon.

In the other direction, northward, the

roadbed swept past a yellow depot and freight shed, curved to miss the tawny adobe town, and pushed toward some low foothills ten miles away. Miles beyond, the rails joined at Dodge City, and every two days an engine pulled a mail car and one coach back and forth to fill the requirements of a mail contract.

This was, Holliday thought, a poor excuse for a railroad's being. In the beginning, Holliday's father had built the line on speculation, to have something to trade. From the beginning it fell in a puddle of red ink and stayed there. Morgansen had been sent out from Chicago to make it pay, and lasted six months. He was a genius, in his own way, but he couldn't beat the Indians, or the Texans, who figured it was better to have no railroad at all than to fight the Indians again.

The second man Holliday hadn't known at all; he'd heard that he had a background of politics, and he'd lasted four months, and the rails continued to gather rust.

All this drove home to Ben Holliday his own sense of unimportance; he was neither a genius nor a politician, yet he was supposed to succeed where they had failed.

He opened his coat because he knew today would be as hot as yesterday; he hadn't known a genuinely cool day since he'd arrived. The tin roof didn't do anything to lessen the bake-oven heat either. On his desk were some letters that had come in on last night's train.

3

He recognized his father's handwriting on one, and Ben Holliday knew without opening it what the gist of it would be. It would be full of advice, and questions, and more advice, and a reminder that there wouldn't be any salary until the line was paying its own way. His oldest brother, Lon, would probably enclose a note; he was always doing that, never writing a letter, just enclosing notes, as though any opinion he had was a fringe comment on what someone else had already said.

Adam, who was only a year older than Ben, had written, and this letter was quickly opened. A cashier's check for three hundred dollars fluttered to the desk, and Ben Holliday let it lie there.

He began to read.

Chicago, May 7, 1882

Dear Brother Ben:

A fantastic bit of luck here. That case I was working on was settled out of court, so I enclose a small check to tide you over until you get control of things. Before you get righteous and indignant, let me say that I now consider having paid you in full for that small book of addresses you left in my care. Your taste in femininity is exemplary; Alice is particularly delightful, and she misses you terribly although I am doing my best to make her forget. I shall probably plunge beyond my financial capabilities in doing so, but I figure it will be worth it.

Brother Lon still puts in his ten hours a day; he's in charge of the Chicago office now and more like Father every day. I hope he succeeds; you know how badly he takes failure, and if he ever does, he's just the kind of silly ass who'd think it fitting to fall on his sword. The rooms in our family 'museum' are as empty as ever; we need a woman here to liven it up, and I've been talking about it to Alice; I must either marry her or drop her before I go broke.

Conclude your business with the Texans as soon as possible and come home, Ben. Really, Friday night poker is not the same without you; I have yet to find another who so consistently loses to me. And stay away from the Indian squaws; I understand they are treacherous in matters of breach of promise.

Affectionately,
Adam

Ben Holliday chuckled and put this letter, and his father's, in his coat pocket, then stepped out of his office. The second floor contained the administrative staff of Midland-Pacific: the timekeeper and accountant shared one office, the freight superintendent and maintenance head another, with the chief telegrapher and the dispatcher together. Well, we'll all be out of a job soon, Holliday thought, and went down the back stairs, which opened into the equipment yard, with the cookshack on the other side. He made his way through mountains of railroad ties and stacked rails and rolls of telegraph wire.

By rule of thumb, he figured Midland-Pacific had about thirty or forty days of life left before the money ran out. After that, it was either pull up the rails or run a train over them and make it pay.

A triphammer banged away in the round house, and he could hear the steam donkey huffing away; and smell the hot metal from the foundry; the sounds were busy, prosperous sounds, full of industry, and he hated to think of it just stopping.

He went into the cookshack and sat at a table near the door, where he could smell the bacon frying and the pitch odor from the tie piles. He ate his breakfast and looked out the door at the rolling stock idle on the yard sidings. Two good engines there, both coal burners, young, full of power, and nowhere to go.

This was the point of thinking he always came back to, that urge to get up steam, give the whistle cord one long pull, and roll out, heading south. That stretch of rusting track beckoned him like the invitation in a women's eyes, almost beyond resistance.

While he was having his coffee, Ollie

Skinner came in, his battered hat respectfully held in his hands. Skinner was fifty some, dry humored, as sun-cooked as the land, and as shiftless as the wind that never quite seemed to stop blowing. 'Mr. Holliday,' he said, 'I found you a couple of fellas who want to see a horse and buggy.'

'How much?' Ben asked.

'Sixty dollars,' Ollie Skinner said. He had a slow Texas drawl in his voice, and his skin was like a piece of old leather that had lain in the sun too long. This was his second year with the railroad, but he wasn't a company man and never would be, for he was a Texan and his thinking was pretty well defined, his opinions already established. Holliday felt a little irritated by Skinner's manner; the man seemed to work for the pay, with no loyalty or feeling, and Holliday always felt that behind Skinner's wrinkled face there was a joke somewhere, and not on himself.

'All right,' Ben said, rising. 'Where are they?'

'By the depot.'

Holliday frowned. 'Couldn't they come here?'

'A man learns to stay in his place,' Skinner said, and went out.

The depot and freight shed sat alone, halfway between the town and the railroad yard, like some unwanted relative. Across the tracks, rows of identical yellow houses were

7

crowded together, railroad owned, built for railroad employees. The houses weren't much, Holliday knew, just three rooms, slab siding, sheet-iron roofs, and cinders for a yard. They needed paint now; this climate was hard on any finish. But there was no money to spare for painting. Although he had never been there, he knew how poor their living standard was; he could see the people from his office window, and hear them on a still day, the children yelling, the women yelling in Polish and German and Italian.

By comparison, the town looked good, and it wasn't much, just a wide dirt street with manure piles attracting flies, and adobe buildings crammed close together, and a few trees carefully tended so that they grew to shady usefulness. It was a rough town in a rough land, quick to spring up and built to do, and that was all.

Do for Texans, Holliday thought, as he approached the depot. It would never do for me.

The two men sat in the shade, and they stood up when Skinner and Holliday approached. The horse and buggy were standing to one side. 'Thet's a purty good rig,' one of the Texans said. He had a hound-lean face and his jaws worked rhythmically on his chew of tobacco. He stood with his hands tucked into the waistband of his jeans, which rode very low on his hips; Holliday expected

8

them to slip off any minute. Both Texans carried revolvers; Holliday felt this was more from custom than necessity, and he eyed them with a certain suspicion because of it.

'A good head,' the other said. He glanced at his partner and jabbed him in the ribs with an elbow. 'Ain't you got nothin' to say, Satchel? Brag him up a little.'

'Heeheehee, well, mister, he's lively, I reckon.'

Holliday looked the buggy over; it seemed sound, although well used. Then he walked around and looked at the horse, a lithe, walleyed brute that kept rearing his head and rolling his eyes.

Satchel said, 'He's just nervous aroun' stranger, mister.'

'He does seem to have spirit,' Ben said.

Satchel's crackling laugh seemed almost uncontrollable. 'You're a good judge of horseflesh there, mister. Heeheeheeheehee-heehee!'

Holliday looked at Ollie Skinner. 'What do you think?'

'I just brung you here.' He took hold of the buggy wheel and gave it a shake. 'Seems solid enough. Worth sixty dollars.'

The horse was unusually active, stamping his feet, throwing his head, and either trying to back up or go forward a little. 'We wouldn't be sellin' him,' Satchel said, 'except that we need the money. Sixty's our bottom price, friend.

9

Take it or leave it.'

'Well,' Ben said, with some hesitation. 'I've got a have a horse and buggy.' He reached into his vest pocket and counted out six ten-dollar gold pieces. 'Give the bill of sale to Skinner.' He stepped into the rig and picked up the reins. 'Whoa there! Whoa now!'

'He jest needs a bit of exercise,' Satchel said smiling. Then he jabbed his friend in the ribs and winked at Ollie Skinner. He picked the revolver from his holster, pointed it straight up, and triggered it.

Ben Holliday, sitting there trying to quiet the horse, thought that the animal had gone from a dead standstill to a dead run in one jump. His feet flew straight out and up and he almost cascaded over the seat. By the time he regained some position of security, the horse was going over the tracks, the buggy flailing along behind like a string-held stick dragged behind a running boy. One of the rear wheels shed its spokes on the rails, and Ben saw the iron-shod rim roll crazily by, and this frightened the horse to renewed frenzy.

They tore wildly through the first row of shacks and the buggy slewed around, the tail end clipping an outhouse with enough force to topple it. Women and children were running out of the shacks and waving, and this didn't improve the horse's disposition.

Holliday was shouting and tugging at the reins and trying to slow the animal, but it was useless. Even the hub with splintered spokes gouging out a trail failed to slow him.

Ahead of him, between two buildings, a slender blond woman was busily washing clothes; she had them strung on a line and turned to see the rig bearing down on her.

'Get out of the way!' Ben yelled, then he was plowing through. The near front wheel struck the washtub and sent it spinning like a big wooden bowl, the water pinwheeling out of it. Then the horse caught the clothesline and the flapping sheets and shirts and underwear drove him completely mad.

Leaving the yard and a swatch of litter, Holliday only hoped that the woman had escaped being trampled; his memory was only of her sprawling, dress flying, then her rolling on the ground.

Ahead of him lay a wash, and the horse took the jump down, but he knew the buggy wasn't going to make it. He felt it hit, the axle fracture, both wheels collapse, and knew the buggy was not going to land right side up. So he left it, pushing with his legs to get clear and trusting to luck for the rest. He hit the dirt and felt the wind jar out of him, then he rolled five or six times and ended in a sitting position in eight inches of muddy water.

The horse kept on going and Ben Holliday didn't give a damn now. He got up slowly, expecting broken bones, but there didn't seem to be any. His only thought was for the woman,

11

and he knew she must be dead or severely trampled.

Quickly he crawled out of the wash and ran back toward the gathering crowd of noisy women and children, picking up clothes and bed sheets that he had been whipped off the line by the horse's speed. They were torn and dirty, and he had quite an armful by the time he got there. The people were so tightly packed that he could not find a way through, then he started to pull at them, saying, 'Pardon me. Please let me through. Let me through, will you?'

Not many understood his words, and they all began to shout at once, and without knowing a word of their respective languages, he was certain they were not complimenting him on his driving skill. Then he saw the blond woman, dirty from being thrown to the ground, and water-soaked from the wheeling tub. She began to push at the people gathered there, driving them away, back to their own homes. And Ben Holliday was relieved, because he hated a public row, and this one was going to be a good one.

He stood there, her ruined laundry in his arms. His coat was completely split up the back seam, and both knees protruded from gaping rents, and he couldn't have got any more mud on him if he'd shared a sow's wallow.

'*Du bist ein Esel!*' the girl shouted. Her

12

anger was as intense as any he had ever seen. Her hair was in disarray and her white blouse was ripped, exposing a shoulder that was delightfully smooth and rounded. Still he expected her to see that this had been an accident; there was no call for her to be so angry, and he just knew that she'd sworn at him.

'What was that you said? What did you call me?'

'I called you an ass! A donkey!' Then she snatched the clothes from him, looked at them in horror, and threw them on the ground. Immediately she burst into tears 'Oh, just look at what you've done! Just look at my clothes, my tub!'

'Well you don't have to bawl about it,' he said. 'I'll buy you a new tub. Look at my wrecked buggy!' He had his hands on his hips now, and his voice rose in volume. She was rather tall, he noticed, a slender, shapely girl with good bones and a real temper. He had never seen eyes so full of fire.

'I'll cry if I want!' Tears rolled down her cheeks, into the dirt streaks there, and she turned and kicked at the clothes and he knew that she pretended she was kicking him. Then she went loose and sat down on the clothes and let her head tip forward, her sobbing shaking her shoulders.

He felt a strong compassion for her and bent and put his hand on her arm. She bit him

13

suddenly, bit him hard, and he yelped and snatched his hand back and, looked at the row of even teeth marks.

'Why, you damned wildcat!' He felt his temper flare like a sudden fire. 'I ought to paddle you where it'll do the most good!' And to show her that he wasn't fooling, he took off his ruined coat and threw it to one side.

She sprang to her feet and faced him, her face inches from his. 'You touch me and I'll make you sorry, you *dummkopf! Warum bist du so dumm*?' She pointed back toward the depot. 'Get out!'

'Won't you let me explain? The horse ran away!'

She struck him with the heels of her hands, holding her arms stiff, and he retreated a step. 'Go on, get out!' She rammed him again. 'Do you hear what I say?' Then she dropped her arms loosely and looked at the clothes as though she couldn't yet believe it.

'I'm sorry,' he said.

'Just leave me alone,' she said, almost begging him.

He hated to leave, with her blaming him. But what did he really expect after turning order into a shambles? He looked around and saw the Texans standing across the tracks, taking it all in; they thought it was a big joke. Ben said, 'Can't I come back later when you're feeling better? We can talk about it then.'

'I don't want you to come back,' she said.

14

Then she looked at him and he was surprised to find her no longer angry. It seemed that she was more defeated now, and this state of mind alarmed him. 'Each time I wash, I tell myself, now Anna, you be careful and not rub too hard and make the clothes last longer. They were the last of my mother's sheets that I brought here from Germany. The last thing of hers that I had left. Now they're gone.' She studied him as though puzzled. 'Why do you stand there and look at me? Do you like to see me cry?'

'No,' Ben said. 'And it would please me if you never had to cry again.' Then he quickly turned and walked across the tracks to where the crowd of Texans stood.

Ollie Skinner was there, his wrinkled face bland and unreadable.

'That hoss could sure run, couldn't it, Mr. Holliday?'

He looked intently at Skinner and resisted the impulse to hit him. 'Where did Satchel and his friend go with my money?'

'A man shouldn't go back on a deal once he's made it,' Skinner pointed out, but then saw that this advice fell on deaf ears. 'In the saloon, I reckon. The story will be worth tellin'.' He glanced at the good citizens from town, then at Holliday. 'You got somethin' on your mind, Mr. Holliday?'

Skinner's amusement solidified Holliday's resolve. He said. 'Come along and see, and afterward pick up your money from the

15

timekeeper. You're fired!'

He left Skinner standing there with a slack jaw and walked toward the head of Comanche's single street. The sun bounced off the adobe walls and shade lay dark and inviting beneath the store overhangs. From the saloon halfway down the street, Holliday could hear the foot stamping and thigh slapping and a whinny of laughter that sounded familiar.

As Holliday passed the marshal's office, the door swung wide and Jim Bender stepped out. He was a tall, blunt-faced man, as tough as a horseshoe and about as flexible in his ways. He wore a white shirt and trousers tucked into his boots and a well-oiled, bone-handled pistol in a crossdraw holster.

He cuffed his hat to the back of his head and said, 'Mr. Holliday, I can't recall ever seein' you look more determined.' His glance traveled back down the street to the group of townspeople who had stopped. 'They had their joke, so why don't you let it go at that?'

'Would you?' Ben asked.

'No,' Bender said. 'But we're different.'

'Tell me how different?' He looked at Bender and waited.

The marshal's young face grew serious. 'Well then, if you've got your hackles up, I'd better go along to keep it fair.'

'Fair for them, or for me?'

A hard tone came into Bender's soft voice. 'Friend, that word only has one meaning for me. Be well if you'd learn that.'

'So far I haven't seen anything to show me,' Ben Holliday said.

He walked on to the saloon, and Jim Bender watched him and waited for the crowd to come along. He held out his hand and it stopped, eyeing him curiously.

'I want Holliday to have all the room he wants,' Bender said. 'Don't make me repeat that.'

One of the Texans scowled. 'Say, are you a railroad man now, Jim?'

'I've spent my life being for nothing,' Bender said. 'Now don't anyone go and mix me up.' He stepped to the street, taking Holliday's route to the saloon.

As Ben mounted the porch, he heard the crackling laugh, 'Heeheeheeheeheehee you should have seen him thar, arms 'n' legs a-flyin', and yellin', *"Whoa!"* as loud as he could. Heeheeheeheeheehee, that hoss hadn't heard whoa in his life.'

A gale of laughter and bar slapping followed, and Ben Holliday got as far as the poker tables before anyone noticed him. Then a hush came over them and Holliday picked up a straight-backed chair, crashed it to kindling on a table, then sorted through the pieces for one that suited him. He selected a leg, a round, heavy piece of ash and stepped toward Satchel and his friend.

The others faded back to make room, and

17

Satchel said, 'Now you ain't got yourself all riled up, have you?'

'No,' Ben Holliday said. 'But it's my turn now. Suppose you put the sixty dollars on the bar.'

Jim Bender stepped through the door and stood just inside, his arms crossed nonchalantly. Satchel looked like a man who didn't know whether to laugh or swear. Finally he said, 'Aw now, you're sore. That's too bad. The next thing you'll be wantin' to fight.'

'Put the money on the bar.'

Satchel smiled, then shook his head, and Ben Holliday hit him across the jaw hinge with the chair leg, and it cracked like a snapped twig. Satchel whipped into the bar and sagged like a sun-wilted flower and he lay with his head against the brass footrail.

His friend looked at him and said, 'That was sudden, warn't it?'

'Where's the money?' Holliday asked.

'I ain't—he's got it.'

'Then take it out of his pocket,' Ben said. He stood there while this was being done, then he threw the chair leg away. 'How do you feel about this, horse trader? Do you want to make another joke?'

'Naw, I've had enough laughin' fer one day,' he said. 'Too hot to fight too. Could I buy you a drink?'

Ben Holliday looked at him and thought that here was a man with more brass than he knew what to do with, and he was on the verge of telling him to go to the devil when Jim Bender eased up quietly and put his hand on Ben's shoulder.

'Sure,' Bender said. 'Why not?' His fingers forced down hard, and Holliday knew enough not to object. Bender's dark eyes were smiling, yet there was a caution there, directed at Holliday. 'You're not going to carry a grudge now, are you, Mr. Holliday?'

'No,' Ben said. 'Like he says, it's too hot.'

The bartender filled the glasses and Ben tossed his off, and it was filled again. 'Let's go sit down,' Bender suggested and they went to a corner table. He took off his hat and ran his fingers through his dark hair. The bartender was upending a bucket of water on Satchel and two men pulled him to his feet while a third stuck the neck of a whisky bottle between his lips. Ben Holliday observed this, and Bender said, 'Disappointed, Mr. Holliday?'

'What do you mean?'

'Well, there isn't much satisfaction in just whacking a man once. Anyway, it was Satchel's idea to sell you the horse, and he got the crack on the head. Too bad you can't solve all your problems that easy.'

'Are you any good as a marshal?' Ben Holliday asked.

Bender pursed his lips. 'It's a sideline with me, when you come right down to it. If the railroad can use a good man who knows

Indians, can figure a Texan eighty per cent of the time, and duck the other twenty, I'm available.'

'If you're serious, maybe something can be done,' Ben said. 'I'll know more in a day or so.'

'You mean, when your accountant comes back?'

Holliday did not bother to hide his surprise. 'You know about it? How?'

'Saw him pumpin' the handcar south,' Jim Bender said. He came forward in his chair and put his arms flat on the table. 'I'd say he went to make peace with the Texans. Right?'

'Not peace exactly,' Ben said. 'The railroad is asking favors.'

'From the Texans?'

'We're giving something in return. Marshal, when Harry Lovell comes back, I'll invite you to the meeting. Until then, I'll be happy to know where I can get a dozen linen bed sheets.'

'Sheets?' Bender frowned, as though this were a joke he hadn't heard. 'Not in Comanche, Mr. Holliday. We're still sleeping on shucks around here. The railroad ain't quite brought civilization here yet.' He grinned. 'Ain't that your stock in trade? Your main-line stump speech? Call it 'land grab' if you want, but we bring churches and schools?' He chuckled. 'Drink up, Mr. Holliday; it's a rough world and this puts a rosy tint to it.'

20

CHAPTER TWO

Ben Holliday returned to his quarters and stripped to the waist to wash away the grime, then realized the hopelessness of it and fetched the tub and took a bath. He was dressing when Ollie Skinner timidly knocked on the door, then came in. Holliday was before the mirror, tying his tie. He said, 'The timekeeper's office is three doors down, on the right.'

'I just came to say that you left your money on the bar.' He held it out as though he wasn't sure whether Holliday would take it or not, and when Ben went on knotting his tie, Skinner edged into the room and laid it on the dresser. Then he stood there, rocking back and forth on his run-over heels. 'You wasn't serious about firin' me, was you, Mr. Holliday?'

'Did I act like I was fooling?'

'Well no, which is what bothers me,' Skinner admitted.

'You're a fool, Skinner,' Holliday said. 'How long do you think I'll put up with your games?' He turned to his writing desk and sat down, drawing paper and pencil to him. He ignored Skinner when he wrote.

Chief   Telegrapher—Midland-Pacific—Dodge City on night train one dozen linen bed sheets . . . Have wife pick out six dresses, light colors, to fit slender woman, about five-six tall . . . Include unmentionables with lace, etc. . . . If you mention this to my father you're fired.

Ben Holliday

He pushed back his chair, folded the message, and started to put it in his pocket. Ollie Skinner said, 'I could drop that off for you before I check out, Mr. Holliday. Be no trouble at all.'

Ben studied him for a moment, then asked, 'Skinner, what the hell am I going to do with you?'

Ollie Skinner seemed genuinely puzzled. 'Sure don't know, Mr. Holliday. To tell you the truth, I'd sure hate to get fired. I ain't done an honest day's work since I hired on two years ago, and now I don't know's I can.' He scratched his thatch of gray hair. 'It sure is a problem fer a man to have, ain't it?'

'I'm sick of you dragging your feet,' Holliday said. Then he handed him the message. 'See that it gets sent right away. Then find me another horse and buggy.'

'Sure will.'

'And Skinner, this time I want to see a *child* leading him, you understand?'

Color came into the old man's face; his expression was contrite. 'Sure am sorry, Mr. Holliday. Then again, I ain't. That was the first

22

stand any you railroad fellas made again' the Texans.' He grinned and clapped his hat on his head solidly. 'You just want anything, Mr. Holliday, just holler.'

'I'm going to holler right now if you don't get the hell out of here.'

After Skinner left, Holliday tidied up a bit, emptied the bath water, and hung up the damp towel. His quarters were on the spartan side, one wooden bedstead, three upholstered chairs, a skimpy rug, a battered writing desk, and a dresser, all handed down from former occupants and all showing signs of much use. Someday, he thought, when Midland-Pacific paid regular and generous dividends, he'd order everything new, the very best money could buy. But until then, he'd like what he had.

Returning to his office, he stood by the corner windows for a time and looked south along the unused roadbed. His concentration seemed to center on a point far down the tracks, then he got a pair of binoculars out of his desk and adjusted them. For a full minute he made his observations through the glasses, then put them away and stepped out to the smaller office across the hall.

Fred Casten, the timekeeper, was bringing his daily pay sheets up to date, and he looked around as Holliday stuck his head in the door. Casten was a quiet man of forty, and half of his life had been spent railroading; he didn't like a young man for a boss and tried hard to hide it, which to Holliday's way of thinking was worse than showing it.

'Harry Lovell is pumping the handcar up the track,' Holliday said. 'I want a meeting of all superintendents in my office in an hour.'

Casten considered it as though he had some say about it, then nodded, and Ben Holiday went down the stairs and walked to the switchyard. The maintenance super came out of the roundhouse, and when he saw Holliday standing by the tracks he walked over. 'Is that Lovell coming back?' He lit a cigar, then held it tightly clamped between his teeth. 'Well, good luck, Mr. Holliday. So far all we're having is bad.'

'A man makes his own luck,' Ben said.

Kisdeen grinned. 'I said that myself, when I was thirty.'

He turned and went back to his job and Ben Holliday waited while the handcar grew larger and finally came to a stop on one of the sidings.

Harry Lovell brushed the dust from his clothes and picked up his coat, and a small leather brief case. He was tucking a rifle in the crook of his arm when Ben Holliday came up. A grin came over Lovell's florid face and he patted the brief case. 'Four signatures, Ben. Is that enough?'

'Yes,' Holliday said, relieved. 'I wanted more, but I can force the others into line now.'

He laughed. 'Get cleaned up, then come to my office. And thanks for a good job, Harry.'

'I was a little disappointed myself,' Lovell said.

They walked back to the administration building together and Lovell went into his room on the lower floor while Ben climbed the stairs to his office. When he sat down behind his desk, he felt good for the first time since he'd arrived. Four signatures; he considered this a good start. A very good start.

Ollie Skinner came back and Ben Holliday sent him right out again, to Comanche to invite Marshal Jim Bender to the meeting. He wasn't sure whether Bender had just been talking through his hat or not, but he was going to find out. And if he wasn't, Ben Holliday was going to hire an important man.

Bender arrived early. He came in and wiped sweat from his face with a large bandana. 'Hell can't be much hotter than this,' he said. 'This morning I promised God I'd quit cussin' if He'd cool it off. Guess He didn't believe me.'

'They say we're judged on past performances,' Holliday said. 'Marshal, what does that job pay you a month?'

'Sixty.'

'I'll pay seventy-five.'

Bender raised his eyebrows. 'Must be a big job.'

'It could work into that,' Holliday said. 'The salary will go up in relation to your value to

25

the railroad.' He leaned back in his chair and studied Jim Bender. 'You've been a puzzle to me. I've never been able to figure out who you're for or against. Have you been walking the fence long?'

'All my life,' Bender said. 'It's easier to be for everything and against nothing, as long as I get what I want.' He shook out his tobacco into a paper and rolled it. 'You think I want to be a small-town marshal all my life?' Jim Bender laughed. 'A town's just a town, Mr. Holliday, just so big and not much chance of gettin' bigger. Now a railroad's different. This line is part of another line, which is part of another. A man could grow and never worry about bumpin' his head against the top. Are you still interested in hiring me?'

'Yes,' Ben Holliday said. 'I'm of the opinion that you'll make a good company man, Jim.'

'I guess there are worse things,' Bender admitted. 'Your man came back, huh?'

'Yes,' Holliday said, 'and with some luck.' He leaned forward and folded his hands tightly together. 'I'm going to take a train south to the end of line. In thirty days I intend to have the rust worn off those rails.'

'And Indian trouble,' Bender said. 'They don't like the railroad. Claim they scare the buffalo, and they ain't going to stand still for it. Sure, they won't bother you, because they can't shoot a train off the track, but they'll raid every ranch house in North Texas to get even.

26

That's how come you're not running trains now; surely you know it. The Texans figure it's simpler to drive cattle than to ship them and fight Indians over it.'

'Do they think this situation can last forever?' Holliday asked. 'The railroad is here to stay, Jim. The Indians have to face that, and so do the Texans. I know they've been fighting Comanches and Apaches for fifty years and they're tired of it. But what if I could run the road without a fight?'

Bender laughed. 'Mr. Holliday, you'd find it easier to walk on water. You don't see that trick very often.'

Footsteps came down the hall, and Holliday's door opened. Harry Lovell came in first with his brief case, and he frowned slightly when he saw Jim Bender sitting there. The others filed in and sat down. and Holliday didn't bother to introduce Bender, since they all knew him by sight. He waved them into chairs, then glanced at Harry Lovell, who was taking papers from his brief case.

These were slid across Holliday's desk, and he studied them carefully for a few minutes. Finally he pushed them aside and swiveled his chair around so he could cock his feet up on an open drawer.

'Kisdeen, if I wanted to take a train south, how soon could a work train leave?'

'As soon as the engineer got steam up, Mr. Holliday.'

27

They all straightened in their chairs and their attention sharpened as they looked at Emil Kisdeen. Ben Holliday said, 'I want every telegraph pole we have loaded, every roll of wire, every glass insulator. A full work crew will be ready to leave tonight.' His glance switched to Matt Donovan, the chief telegrapher. 'Get me four telegraphers, Matt. And have their gear with them because they won't be coming back for a while.'

'Just what the divvil's going on?' Donovan asked.

'We're going to run a railroad,' Ben Holliday said. 'You all knew that Mr. Lovell went to the end of track, and now I'll tell you what for. The Texans have refused to ship on our railroad because they all believe we'll stir up the Indians, then stand back while they fight them for us. Until they change their minds, our rolling stock will stay on sidings. So my first concern has been to convince the ranchers that the railroad is ready to stand shoulder to shoulder with them in any fight that comes up. I sent Harry south with a proposition: the railroad will set poles and string wires to any ranch who uses our line on a contract basis. A telegrapher will stay at the ranch, and at the first sign of trouble he'll let us know and a train will be dispatched with horses and men and guns to help the Texans. We've got four outfits signed up, gentlemen. It's enough to start operation on, at a profit.

'It sounds good,' Jim Bender said. 'But tell me somethin'. What about the ones who didn't sign anything? Who the hell helps them out when the Indians start raidin'? The Comanches ain't going to care who's with you and who ain't.'

'You've touched on the heart of the answer,' Holliday said. 'Gentlemen, those who have not signed a contract with us will have no choice but to join us. Without the telegraph, they're wide open to more trouble than they can handle. And to get a telegraph, they've got to ship on our railroad. They've got to join or get licked.' He smiled. 'Now before anyone howls about what a dirty trick this is, let me remind them that we're fighting for our lives, and for the good of the country. As soon as possible, I want to put down a siding about fifty miles south of here, with a full crew there all the time, to bring them closer to any trouble that develops. It'll cost money, but if we start shipping, it won't be long before we pull out of the red.'

'We can't afford much expansion now,' Lovell pointed out. 'As it stands, we have finances for forty-three days.'

'By then I'll be running steady trains,' Ben Holliday said. 'Gentlemen, we have to make the big effort now. We can't afford to wait. If we fail, then we'll do a good job of that too.'

'Only one thing bothers me,' Bender said. What's going to keep the Comanches from pulling that wire down as fast as you can string it?'

'I've given that some thought too,' Holiday said. 'According to Skinner, the Indians make medicine for everything. If it's good medicine, they make wars and go hunting and think that they've got all the luck on their side. But when the medicine is bad, they keep pretty much in line. So I think we ought to make some bad medicine for the Indians.'

'It's going to have to be real bad,' Bender said.

'I'll let you be the judge,' Ben said. 'Donovan, I want you to rig up something with the telegraph wires that'll shock the hell out of anyone who touches it. Bender, I want you to go south and ask all the Indians to come to a big talk and a demonstration of the wire. Then I want to invite them to touch the wire and get a jolt. Then we'll touch it after a switch has been opened, and get none at all.'

'I can go you one better than that,' Donovan said. 'A switch would have to be hid and a man there to throw it off and on. We could all wear rubber boots and be insulated from the wire.'

Holliday looked at all of them. 'Any comments?'

Jim Bender began to laugh. 'Ben, you're a sneaky bastard, but I'll go along with you.'

'When can you leave?'

'Tonight.'

'Fine,' Holliday said. 'Casten, put Bender on

30

the payroll. Seventy-five a month. Kisdeen, you'd better check with me before you pull out with the work train. I'll have maps for both of you. For the meeting, I think the junction of the telegraph wires will do fine. It's open country there, and we can rig up all the wires so the Indians will understand that this isn't just something special.'

'I don't know what else you'd call it,' Lovell said. He closed his brief case. 'Mr. Holliday, this is one hell of a way to run a railroad.' Then he smiled and got up. 'However, if it gets a train on the track, it's better than the other two did. I'll make up a cost sheet to send to your father.'

'The only thing I want to send him,' Ben said, 'is an operating sheet. He knows the line is going broke, so anything else along that line is old information rehashed.' He tapped his finger on the desk. 'In twenty days, gentlemen, I want cattle cars coming into this siding loaded.'

'That's pushing it pretty hard,' Kisdeen said 'I don't think all the wire will be strung by then.'

Holliday picked up the papers Lovell had given him. 'Lazy T has sixteen hundred head ready for shipment. You run your wires there, and when the telegrapher tests the line I want those cattle loaded. Then you take your work train north about twelve miles and string a wire to Box X, and so on down the line. For

Christ's sake, do I have to work out all the details?'

Ben got up and jammed his hands deep into his pockets, then stood by the window and observed the roundhouse activity. 'Lovell expected this job, and he hasn't gotten over his disappointment yet. The others, well, they've already admitted to themselves that we're licked and are counting the days until we pull up the rails and go back East.' Then he turned and looked at Bender. 'I don't want to go back. My father, if he knew what was going on, would roar like a bull and tell me that never in his fifty-nine years had he heard of a railroad being run this way. And he'd be right. Lon, my oldest brother, is a corporation man, and he'd cuss me out for forgetting my obligation to the stockholders, and scold me in a high-finance sort of way because everything in his life is reduced to profit and loss. My other brother, Adam, is a lawyer, and he'd want to talk about all the possible litigation involved, but he'd admire me for getting into this mess without even half trying.'

'I'd like to know him,' Jim Bender said. 'Tell me, how come your old man sent you here, Ben?'

'Because my father firmly believes that every man has to experience failure before he can appreciate success,' Holliday said. 'So he bought up twenty-eight per cent of the stock; it only cost him a few cents on the dollar, then

32

gave it to me and told me to make it worth something, if I could.'

'Mmmm, well it's one way of looking at the world,' Bender admitted. 'What's he going to say if you carry this off?

'He'll like it,' Holliday said. 'Above all else, he admires success.' Then he sat down, a worried frown creasing his forehead. 'Of course there's more to it than just appeasing the Texans and fooling the Indians. Midland-Pacific is in bad financial shape. It would have to operate well for at least six months before she could see the top of the hole she's in. And another four months before any kind of a dividend could be declared.' He shook his head sadly. 'She's a broke railroad, Jim, and there's damned little hope of any new blood being pumped into her.' He pulled a ten-day-old New York paper from his desk and slapped it with his hand. 'To get more money, you have to sell stock, and Midland-Pacific stock has about as much value as wallpaper. I could buy any of it for sixty cents a share. If I had the sixty cents.'

Jim Bender's eyes were veiled and his voice was soft when he said, 'Seems to me that someone around here, who could see that the railroad might make it, could buy up a hog's share, hold it a while, and amass himself quite a hunk of money.' He got up and shifted his pistol to a more comfortable position. 'I'll have to think on it.'

33

'Stop by before you leave,' Holliday suggested.

'I'll do that,' Bender said, and went out.

During the next hour, Holliday cleaned up some paperwork that he had neglected. Skinner came around with a telegram from the Dodge City operator; stating that the shipment would be on the night train, and asking what the devil was going on there. Holliday wrinkled the telegram and threw it in the wastebasket.

He wasn't quite sure how he'd present the German girl with the sheets and things; she might even resent it and create another row. Perhaps, he thought, it would be better if he just sent them over with Lovell or someone. Still, taking them himself was going to be half the pleasure, and he was curious to see her with a clean face.

Most of the day was spent in the yard or roundhouse where the work train was being loaded. A steam donkey hoisted poles and wire rolls onto flatcars, and the crews were being made up, and a cook's car was stuffed with provisions before hooking it in front of the caboose.

Holliday skipped his noon day meal; he was too busy to eat, and he had a late supper, not bothering with it until Jim Bender came and went, heading south with a pack horse. The work train pulled out and it was a good sight to see the engine belching fire and smoke, and just listen to the rattle of the cars fade off into the night. This was what he had been working for, and he felt a little closer to some results; he felt impatient for the day when he could wire north a financial and operation report that wasn't all bad. And when he thought about it, he had to laugh, for in his mind he could visualize his father's reaction, a bellow of surprise, a moment of disbelief, then the half-grudging acknowledgment that 'the boy's done it—'

It would be a good thing, Holliday thought, and walked to his quarters. There he found the door ajar and the lamps lighted, and he paused just outside the door, wondering who was there. He pushed open the door and the hinges squeaked, and with a startled leap the blond German girl got out of her chair.

'I—the man let me in,' she said. 'I don't know his name.'

'Skinner,' Ben Holliday said. 'Sit down. I didn't mean to startle you.' Her hair was braided now, and coiled into a bun on the back of her head, and she stood with her hands folded before her like a child who has been instructed to go cut a switch. She wore a white blouse and a dark skirt and no jewelry except a brooch at her throat. 'I don't even know your name,' he said.

'Anna. Anna Neubauer.'

'Sit down, Anna. I'm Ben Holliday.'

'I know,' she said softly. Then she sat down

35

and he walked to the door and looked up and down the hall. He saw Skinner leaning against the far end. 'Come here.' When Skinner came up, Holliday put his hand on the old man's shoulder. 'Go on over to the cookshack and bring back some coffee.'

'It was all right, me lettin' her in, wasn't it?'

'Yes. Go on now.' Then he turned back into the room; she was watching him intently, and he wondered what to say. 'Will you let me tell you how sorry I am about ruining your clothes?' He grinned. 'And I didn't mean what I said about taking you over my knee.'

Color came into her cheeks. 'You make it hard to say what I came to say. When I called you an—an ass, I didn't know who you were.'

'Well, I can be an ass at times. My brothers would tell you that.'

'But it was wrong to call the boss such a name,' she said. Then she picked up a wrapped bundle and put it on the table. 'This is your coat. I took it away from some boys who were playing with it. There were some letters, but someone had already opened them. I'm sorry I didn't find it sooner.'

He broke the string and took the letters from the inside pocket; there were enough finger smudges on them to convince him they had been well looked over. 'Thanks for bringing them. I've sent Skinner for coffee. You'll stay and have some, won't you?'

'Is it all right?'

36

He frowned. 'Is what all right?'

'To drink coffee with the boss?'

He laughed and reached for her hand, then remembered the last time he'd tried that and pulled his hand back. She caught the meaning of the gesture and quickly clapped a hand to her mouth; her expression was one of chagrin.

'I forgot about that!'

'Well, I haven't,' Holliday said, meaning it as a joke.

But she didn't take it that way at all. 'I told my father what I said. He will leave tomorrow.'

'Leave? What the devil for?'

'Because he is too proud to be fired,' Anna said.

'Now wait a minute,' Ben said, sitting down across from her. 'Anna, I'm not going to fire anyone. And surely not your father for something that was my fault.'

She regarded him with wide eyes. 'You're not? But I called you an ass, and bit your hand.' She shook her head. 'I thought—'

'You thought wrong,' Ben Holliday said. Then he leaned back and laughed. 'Anna, what other foolish notions do you have?'

'To me it isn't foolish,' she said. 'In Germany, we do not swear at the boss or bite his hand. But I've never seen a boss before.'

Skinner came back with the coffee; he brought the tray in and placed it on the table, then acted as though he'd appreciate an invitation to sit. Ben said, 'You can take it back tomorrow.'

'Huh? Oh, sure.' He went out and down the back steps, and Ben Holliday could hear him grumbling clear to the bottom of the landing. He poured the coffee, then said, 'I made a wreck out of your washing, In the morning I'll send Skinner over with a new tub.'

'You don't have to.'

'What'll you do without a tub?'

'Borrow from Mrs. Bartocci, who lives next door.'

'You're too proud to borrow,' Ben said. 'You'll get a new tub in the morning.' He drank some of his coffee and looked at her. She was a very attractive girl, twenty some, with a face a bit squarish, and lips that were soft and long. She caught him staring, and he covered it up by saying, 'I noticed that you speak English with hardly a trace of accent. Where did you learn that?'

'In night school in Chicago. My father worked for the railroad there.' She made descriptive motions with her hands. 'In the foundry he makes things of wood and sand, then parts for the trains are made from hot metal.'

Holliday thought a moment. 'Is he a big man with a stomach and a mustache drooping to his chin?'

Anna Neubauer laughed. 'He drinks too much beer, but he works hard, so I say nothing about the beer.' She sighed wistfully. 'Someday

I say that he won't have to work so hard, but I really don't believe it. It is like my sheets; I'm a fool to think they will last forever.'

'You'll get other sheets, Anna.'

'But they won't be the same.'

'No, we can never have things the same. Every day there's a change, a little more wear somewhere. We've got to figure on the wear, Anna.'

'I know.' She finished her coffee and put the cup aside before standing up. 'You're nice. But I knew that this morning when you gathered up my things and brought them to me. I'm sorry I was too angry to see it, and tell you.'

'I'm glad you came here, Anna.'

'And I am too, now,' she said. He offered her his hand and she took it and he held hers a little longer than was proper, but didn't care and didn't think she cared either.

'Could I walk you home?'

She shook her head. 'It would cause the neighbors to talk. And they are not always kind in what they say.'

'Well, at least to the bottom of the stairs then,' he said, taking her arm. At the bottom of the landing he held her arm to keep her from just disappearing in the darkness. He thought of telling her that he was going to replace the things he had ruined, then decided not to; it would give him an excellent excuse to call on her.

'I have to go,' she said softly.

He relaxed his grip and she slipped from his fingers and was gone. He stood there for a moment, then turned to go back up the stairs. From the shadows near the end of the building, Ellie Skinner said, 'Some things just end too quick, don't they?'

Holliday was annoyed to find the man there, then he laughed. 'Come on up and tell me a lot of lies about yourself and the state of Texas.'

Skinner followed him, and once he got into the room he flopped in a chair and stretched out his legs. 'If I told you about myself, it would be so plumb excitin' you wouldn't believe it. And I ain't got enough years left to tell you all about Texas.' He raised his disgraceful hat in a mock salute. 'However, I feel plumb privileged to be a part of this here vast enterprise of yours, Mr. Holliday.'

Ben frowned good-naturedly. 'Ollie, are you turning into a company man or something?'

'Well, let's put it this way. You're the first boss I've had on this job who didn't treat me like somethin' the cat dragged in. You got a style, Mr. Holliday. Don't know rightly what it is, but you got a style. A genuine wind cutter and a dog howler.' He smacked his lips several times. 'Say, you don't happen to keep any hard liquor about, do you?'

CHAPTER THREE

Just before noon, Ben Holliday walked from his office to the depot to meet the night train from Dodge City; it rattled into the station amid a flurry of swirling cinders and a hiss of brakes. A small crowd of passengers waited in the shade of the depot, and some local freight was stacked for loading. The single coach emptied quickly, just a few local businessmen and a young army officer in a uniform still bearing packing-box wrinkles. The others walked away, but he stood there looking around as though he didn't think much of any of it.

The door of the baggage car was opened and some freight was loaded on handcarts while a three-man cavalry detail from Fort Elliot waited for the mail. The young officer glanced at them briefly, then came over to Holliday.

'I'm Lieutenant Gary, and the conductor tells me this is as far as the train goes.' He was a young man, crisp in manner, with the sharp hone of Academy training much in evidence. His face was long and rather thin, and a downy mustache was bravely trying to mature on his upper lip.

'This is the end of the line, Lieutenant. But nevertheless, welcome to Texas.'

41

'A dubious pleasure, I can assure you,' Gary said. 'Is there a decent hotel in town?'

'If you consider a lumpy mattress and a few sand fleas decent,' Holliday said. 'Excuse me. I have some baggage to pick up.' He smiled and walked over to the express car. 'George, have you got a package for me?'

The express agent handed down a wrapped bundle. 'I heard you're keeping a woman, Mr. Holliday.'

Holliday grinned. 'How would you like to be working for the Arkansas line?' He signed the express agent's book and turned back to the depot where shade lay cool and inviting along the wall. The young officer was still walking about, apparently undecided about what to do. After observing him for a moment, Ben Holliday left the shade, walked around the back of the train, and crossed over to railroad town, carrying the package.

The children were yelling and two boys were throwing cinders at each other, while around them an excited group urged them on. Holliday walked around them, but a small boy and his sister ran after him.

'Hey, meester!' He stopped and looked at the boy, eight or so, dark, with wavy black hair and the deepest brown eyes he had ever seen. The boy grinned. 'Meester, you want see my seester t'row opp?' He took Holliday's sleeve and pulled it. 'For nickel, she t'row opp for you.'

Then a woman ran out of one of the shacks and came up and slapped the boy and yelled at him in Italian; Holliday walked on to Anna Neubauer's house, his step quicker now, as though he only wanted to do what he had to do and get out.

Skinner had already taken the tub over; it sat by her door, full of water to swell the cedar staves. He shifted the bundle and knocked, and Anna opened the door, a fleeting surprise on her face.

'May I come in?' Ben asked.

'Ja bitte herein.' Then she laughed. 'Yes, please.' She stepped aside for him, then closed the door.

Without consciously thinking about it, Ben Holliday had schooled himself on showing no reaction to her poverty-level dwelling; from the outside it was a shack with paint peeling off the sides and the tar-paper roof curling along the edges. And from the outside he had pre-judged the inside, so what he found rattled him completely.

The furniture, every stick of it, had been carefully packed to endure the journey from Germany without damage, and all of it was black walnut, heavily carved, built to endure generations of use without showing a trace of deterioration. A glass-fronted cupboard held her dishes, fine bone china, and silver that could only have been handcrafted by a master.

She watched him look around, then said,

43

'My grandmother was a rich woman, Mr. Holliday. These were things I could not leave behind, but I often wish that I had.' She turned to the stove where a coffeepot warmed. 'Nearly all of the women here are poor, and I no longer invite them into the house. It only makes them angry, and they won't understand that these things were given to me.' Her shoulders rose and fell. 'Thank you for the tub, but there'll be talk.'

'As much as I hate to say it, there's going to be more talk.' He laid the bundle on the table, and she looked questioningly at it. 'Go ahead, open it.'

Before she touched it he knew she'd untie the string and save both that and the wrapping paper. She gasped when she saw the sheets and dresses and underclothes, and she ran her hands over the folded sheets for a moment.

'What can I say, they're so nice? There will be gossip about me when I hang them on the line, but it'll be worth it, I think.'

'I hope you can explain it to your father,' Ben said, smiling. 'In Chicago, I gave a girl a pair of stockings.' He rolled his eyes toward the ceiling. 'It almost became a scandal. I'm sure this will make trouble for you.'

'It's something I'm used to,' she said. 'Will you stay for coffee?'

He shook his head. 'No doubt the ladies here are keeping track of the time from when I entered. Which makes it important for me to

44

leave early.' He opened the door and stood there a moment. 'How do I cross from where I live to here, Anna?'

'Are you sure you want to?'

'I think so.' He raised both hands and looked at them. 'How does one break down walls he can't see, but knows are there?' Then he closed the door and walked back across the tracks and on to his office.

The sun was making an oven of it, and he took off his coat and tie and rolled his sleeves. Ollie Skinner came in a few minutes later with Holliday's shredded coat rolled into a untidy ball.

'You want me to throw this out, Mr. Holliday?'

'Yes. Wait! There are a couple letters in the pocket' Skinner felt and patted the cloth until he heard paper rustle, then took them out and laid them on Holliday's desk.

After he went out, Ben picked up the letter from his father and gave it a tardy reading.

Chicago, May 6, 1882

Dear Ben:

At hand I have a communication from an attorney in Dodge City, who represents local interests. He has made a bona fide offer to purchase Midland-Pacific. I don't know why he got in touch with me, unless he was unaware that you are now chairman of the board. But I think this is unlikely. For

45

some reason or another he does not want to do business with you.

Have you been alienating these people? God knows they're uncooperative enough.

I've studied this offer at length, and Adam has looked it over, and in spite of the fact that he disagrees with me, I believe it is an answer to a sticky problem. M-P has lost money at an alarming rate, and I believe will continue to do so in spite of any effort you might make. Sincerity does not count in this business, Ben. Only results, and I fear there will be precious little of those.

Naturally the sale will leave you nothing; the common stockholders will have to be paid off first, and their share will be pitifully small. But you'll be out from under it with a clean bill of health, and you can come back to Chicago; there is plenty to do here.

Since I've already approved of this offer, I will not enclose the papers. Of course, legally you are the chairman of the board and can do as you wish, but don't fly in the face of providence and sound judgment, Ben. I urge you to write me your letter of acceptance at your earliest opportunity.

Midland-Pacific is broke, dead, finished. Bury her without tears and take the last train to Dodge and home.

Your father,
Julius

Holliday laid the letter on his desk and sat with his chin in his hands, considering this unexpected turn of events. The fact that there was a buyer for the line surprised him, but after thinking a moment, it made a lot of sense. His father had started that way, buying a defunct line for a few cents on the dollar and making it pay handsomely. That was evidently someone's idea here.

But who?

He didn't have a chance to think about it, for Skinner came back. 'Some sojer wants to see you,' he said. 'Says he talked to you at the depot.'

'All right, send him in,' Holliday said. 'And go over to the cookshack and bring back some sandwiches and some coffee.'

Skinner went out and Lieutenant Gary stepped in, his manner hesitant. 'I'm sorry to intrude, but they told me at the depot that you run the railroad.'

'Have a chair. Run it?' Holliday smiled. 'You're very generous, Lieutenant. However, you have problems of your own, I'm sure.'

'Mainly, getting to Fort Elliot. It's my understanding that the roadbed runs within eight miles of the post.'

'Yes, to the west, and terminates about twenty miles beyond, at a water tank, a telegraph shack, and a small bunkhouse. Is Fort Elliot your assignment?'

Gary nodded. 'And I'm going to be late for

it, damn it. A man's first duty and he has to botch it.' He sighed. 'I spent too much time with my sisters, I'm afraid, and did not take into consideration the abominable traveling conditions.' He crossed one leg over the other and put his hands on his knee. 'I was told that you sent a train south last night. May I ask how far?'

'To the end of track.'

Gary swore softly, in a gentlemanly manner. 'I've been missing connections since St. Louis!' He slapped his knee. 'I don't suppose there's another train—no, I thought not. Damn, but there is an ominous tone to a man being tardy for his first assignment.'

Ben Holliday was thinking about this when Skinner came back, a tray of sandwiches and a pot of coffee in hand. Gary said, 'That looks good. I haven't had anything since supper last night.'

'Help yourself,' Holliday said. 'Skinner, I think I'll take the handcar to the end of track. See that it's ready in about an hour.'

'You aint goin' alone, are you?' Skinner asked.

'I thought I'd take Lieutenant Gary along.' He smiled at Ollie Skinner. 'Well, don't look like that. I can pump a handcar. And get me a rifle and some shells from the freight office. I'll take care of the rest.'

'All right,' Skinner said, his tone predicting dire things to come.

After he left, Lieutenant Gary said, 'If you're doing this for me,—I'

'I can't run a railroad sitting down,' Holiday told him. 'We can pump ten miles an hour, spend the night on the prairie, and leave you with only an eight-mile walk to the post.' He bit into one of the sandwiches. 'I thought a military escort was supposed to meet you officers.'

'Likely there was one, at Tascosa, a week ago,' Gary said. 'I'm really that far behind, I'm sorry to say.' He shrugged and picked up his cup of coffee. 'I tried to send a wire, but the telegraph only runs to here. Oh, what a dismal state of affairs.'

'I thought the army had its own signal service.'

'Of course, heliograph and dispatch riders.' He snorted in disgust. 'But not telegraph, except when near the main line. You say the post is eight miles from your telegraph lines? What a shame they're not tied into it.'

'Take it up with your congressman the next time you're in Washington. Poles and wire and insulators cost money. Who's going to foot the bill? The railroad? We built this line out of our own pocket, for railroad business.' He jerked open a desk drawer. 'I've three letters there from Colonel Dawson asking if we'd string wire to Fort Elliot. We would, only he hasn't the authority or the money to pay the bill.'

'You're certainly not much of a visionary,'

49

Gary said frankly.

'How so?' He got up and took his coffee to the windows and stood there, sipping it and looking out.

'Fort Elliot's function is to keep the Indians in line, Mr. Holliday. It seems to me that it would serve your function admirably if you put the line in at your expense. You railroaders are always stirring up the Indians. A telegraph wire would bring the army in a hurry.'

Holliday turned and looked at him for a moment, then came back to his desk and sat down. 'Mr. Gary, I assume that you are a genius.'

'I was sixty-third in my class,' Gary said. 'There were seventy-one, all told.' He frowned pleasantly. 'Did I say something bright? By golly, I'm due for a change, you know.'

'Finish your sandwich and coffee,' Holliday said, picking up his coat. He stepped out and went down the hall to Dan Rawlins's office. The freight superintendent was reading an old newspaper and he put it away quickly when Holliday came in, as though ashamed at getting caught. 'Have you made up that string of empty cattle cars yet?' Rawlins handed him a sheet and Holliday looked at it, then gave it back. 'When the first cattle train rolls out for Dodge, deadhead six flatcars. Tell Lovell to handle the paper work, but I want all the poles and wire Western Union can spare. Enough to string an additional eight miles.'

'All right, but who's going to pay for it, Mr. Holliday? We can't afford those kind of expenditures.' He scratched a day-old-beard stubble. 'I hate to remind you, but everyone knows we're broke, or close to it. We don't have enough credit to buy a ton of coal.'

'Do you play poker, Mr. Rawlins?'

'Well, I do now and then. But I'm not crazy about the game.'

'You should play with my brother, Adam; he can bluff the money out of a cardshark's pocket.' Holliday slapped Rawlins on the shoulder. 'I'm not bad at bluffing myself.'

He whistled on the way back to his office, then looked in Donovan's office. The telegrapher was cat napping, his feet on the desk, and Holliday shook him awake. 'Curly, are you friendly with the Dodge City operator?'

'Why, sure. We used to work connecting shifts for Western Union.'

'Then I got a bit of gossip for you to pass along to him. Be worth three drinks at least.' He bent forward to speak softly, and glanced over his shoulder before he really came out with it. 'We've got some fresh money, Curly. Over a hundred thousand dollars from a Dodge City investor.' He clapped the man on the back. 'We're out of the hole. And I've been thinking about a raise to celebrate.'

He went out while the man was still a little open-mouthed over it, and before he stepped into his office, Holliday puffed his cheeks and blew out a long breath. The telegrapher was asking for a clear signal, and Holliday stepped in and closed the door.

Gary was smoking a cigar and he said nothing, and Holliday was glad because he wanted a chance to think this out. He had no doubt that there was already some talk in Dodge about a buying interest in Midland-Pacific; you just couldn't keep those things absolutely quiet, especially among the bankers and money men. And this bit of nothing Curly was spreading would catch on, enough, Holliday hoped, to convince the manager of Western Union that this shaky railroad was good for five carloads of poles and ten spools of wire. Holiday knew that there would be a lot of nosing around to find out just how true the rumor was, but he knew investors; they were all hunch players with big ears from keyhole listening. His own father had made his first million by taking advantage of rumors and getting there first with the right things.

'Are you working on a plan to assassinate the President?' Gary asked, drawing Holliday's attention back with a snap.

Ben laughed. 'I'm playing big business with a busted flush. Do you have any luggage?'

'Sitting by the bottom landing.'

'I'll meet you there after I change clothes,' Holliday said. 'Skinner ought to have the handcar ready.'

In his quarters, he changed to some old hunting clothes he'd brought along, and laughed silently while he put them on. His notion, before he came here, was that he would have time to indulge in a few gentlemanly activities, like grouse hunting, and perhaps a buffalo hunt. As it turned out, he had twenty days of messed-up paper work to sort through before he even got a vivid picture of the railroad's ills. There was little time for thought of gentlemanly pursuits.

He found Gary waiting, and they walked together to the switchyard. Skinner was there, sitting in the sparse shade. He had some gear of his own stowed on the handcar, and Holliday looked at it.

'Where do you think you're going?'

'Along,' Skinner said. He held up his hands. 'Before you get to yellin' at me, let me just say that it ain't goin' to hurt you none, and it may do you a bit of good. I know this country. It would pay you to listen once in a while. That there chairman of the board thing don't make you that smart.'

Lieutenant Gary frowned; he disapproved of this kind of talk from a hired man. But this was railroad business and he kept out of it. Finally Holliday said, 'Let's go then. Gary and I'll pump. We don't want you keeling over from overwork, Skinner.'

They pushed the handcar past the switch, and while it was coasting the two men laid their weight on the handles and got up a little speed. Skinner sat on the bow, his Sharps rifle crossways on his knees.

It was a good feeling, the dripping sweat from Holliday's face soaking his shirt, and he liked the sound of the wheels clacking over the rail joints, eating the miles away, moving along briskly southward in a flat, dun-colored country with hardly a break in it. The string of telegraph poles marched by, and if a man wanted to count them and do a little mental arithmetic, he could calculate his rate of travel very accurately.

Skinner spelled them in turn, and they didn't stop at all until the sun was well down. They left the handcar on the track and camped near the roadbed. Skinner put together a fire, gathering the heavy stems of brush for fuel. The meal was mainly bacon and soggy pancakes, followed by coffee so strong you could etch copper with it. Gary brought out three cigars, and this pleased Skinner, who had a taste for them but was too tight with a nickel to buy his own.

'When you report to Colonel Dawson,' Holliday said, 'It might soften the effect of your tardiness if you mention that you'd talked me into building the telegraph line to the post.'

Skinner raised his head and looked disgustedly at Ben Holliday. 'That's a fool move. Ain't you got enough troubles without

54

bringing in the army?'

'I never thought of it until Mr. Gary mentioned it, but it's the smartest advice I ever took. Skinner, our position's a lot stronger with the Texans if we string wire to Fort Elliot. It's like Mr. Gary says: the army is there to keep the Indians in line.'

Ollie Skinner chuckled, but Lieutenant Gary didn't see the humor in it. 'The military,' he said, 'is not an instrument to be used by civilian enterprise, Mr. Holliday.'

'It is if you want a telegraph,' Ben pointed out.

'I see. If I'd known that—'

'You'd still need the telegraph,' Holliday said. 'Now before you accuse anybody of pulling a sneaky, try to see my position. If this railroad operates, army supplies will only be eight miles from the post, and instead of freighting them in on the stage road to Tascosa, the army will get them at much less rate. You're forgetting about the contract the government has with all railroads: men and material transported at a rock-bottom rate. Don't expect to get anything for nothing. It never works.'

'I'm goin' to inform Colonel Dawson of these ramifications,' Gary said.

Ben Holliday laughed. 'He already knows, and then some. The railroad is going to make his job easier.'

'And tougher,' Gary said. 'I heard about all

55

the Indian trouble you've stirred up.'

'Then look at it this way,' Holliday said. 'If we didn't stir up the Indians, you wouldn't have a job to do.'

Skinner stopped puffing on his cigar. 'Sonny, don't argue with him; it don't do any good. His old man's one of them big moguls, and his brothers are swindlers from the word go. And most of it's rubbed off on him.'

Gary said, 'Are you going to let him talk to you like that?'

Holliday waved it aside. 'All Texans are windbags, Mr. Gary. Now get some sleep.' He turned to his blankets and stretched out, using his folded hands for a pillow. 'Skinner, how are the rattlesnakes around here?'

'Friendly. Come right up and share your blankets. But don't roll on 'em. Makes 'em grouchy.'

'Good advice,' Holliday said blandly.

'Say, he's just joking, isn't he?' Gary asked.

'Don't go walkin' along the tracks at night,' Skinner said. 'You'll find out then whether I'm jokin' or not. They like to lay against the rails to keep warm.'

'I think I'll sleep on the handcar,' Gary said, and got his blankets. Skinner chuckled and lay there, his cigar end glowing redly for a time. Then he snuffed it out and went to sleep.

The dawn sunlight woke them, and Skinner booted first Holliday, then Garry. 'Up! Up!' he said. 'Come on, up!'

Gary came to a sitting position and rubbed his backside. 'By God, I'm not used to being woke like that,' he said. 'Don't you ever hear of shaking a man, Skinner?'

'Did that one time: Got my hand bit.' He rubbed his hands together. 'Let's get pumpin'. Who's going to take the other handle?'

'On an empty stomach?' Gary said. He stood there while Holliday and Skinner rolled the blankets and put them on the handcar. Then Gary sighed and took a handle while Skinner pushed it into motion.

'If I had him in my outfit,' Gary said, meaning Skinner, 'I'd have him in the guardhouse.'

'And I doubt if it'd hold him,' Holliday said. He pointed to a spot far out on the prairie. 'What's that?'

Skinner, who was riding backwards, turned his head for a look. He squinted his eyes for a moment, then said, 'Oh, oh. Here, you pump.' He picked up his rifle and sat on the prow. 'Buffalo. Not many. Fifty-sixty maybe. Movin' this way too.'

'Can't we outrun them?' Gary asked.

'No, you can't,' Skinner said. 'Maybe we don't have to, though. Just keep up that steady pace, gents. Or a little faster, if you've a mind to. Speed at a time like this won't hurt nothin'.' He took out the stale cigar stub he'd saved from last night, bit off the charred end, then chewed the rest. From his coat pocket he took out a box of .50-125 Sharps Express cartridges and held four of them in the palm of his left hand.

Holliday, who had a good view facing in the direction of their travel, could see that the buffalo herd was traveling a course converging on their own; they were likely to meet up ahead somewhere, and it wasn't good to think about.

He and Gary increased the cadence of their pumping and rattled along, only now he could no longer hear the clack of the wheels; the steady drum of hoofs closed it out. Yet he could feel the vibration at each rail joint, but only for a while as the approaching herd set up a vibration that made track and rail bed tremble. Gary's eyes were getting glassy and both men were breathing hard, yet they did not slacken their exertions.

Holliday could see clearly the humped backs and massive heads and the thick, filthy pelts, and the odor of the herd came to him strong and frightening. There was a time when only thirty yards separated them, then they passed on and the herd crossed the tracks at an angle and ran on to the other side and away from them.

They slowed somewhat but continued to pump for a mile or so, then sat down and let the handcar coast to the stop. The herd went on, to the west of them, the sounds of their passage dying until it was only a thunder rumble in the distance.

Skinner was sweating. He put his cartridges and rifle away and spat tobacco. 'Close, that was. Can't take it much closer. Gives a man a bad heart, too much of that.'

This joking admission of fright from Ollie Skinner was unnerving for Gary and Ben Holliday. They drank from their canteens, then Ben said, 'Why the hell didn't you shoot? Or did you forget to load it?'

'No sense in it,' Skinner said. 'I didn't want to take a chance on turnin' 'em. They could have turned into us.'

'How often does a man run into something like that?' Gary asked.

'Enough to make him old at thirty-five,' Skinner said. He squinted and studied the farthest reaches of the prairie. 'There's Indians about. They got that herd running.'

'I thought I saw blood on a couple of cows,' Holliday said.

Skinner grinned and slapped his leg. 'By golly, you ain't as blind as I thought. Yep, you saw blood all right. Some brave put a .44 into her, or an arrer, then broke it off feelin' fer the life.'

'What's he talking about?' Gary said.

'Feelin' fer the life?' Skinner smiled. 'It's brave doin's, sonny. When they hunt with arrers, they sink a shaft, then ride alongside, lean from the horses, and with their hand shove the arrer home, guidin' it into the heart

59

or lung. Call it feelin' fer the life.'

'It sounds like a damned good way to die,' Gary said flatly, considering it foolish.

'Death ain't nothin' to an Indian,' Skinner said. 'Just an event, like bein' born. It's what's in-between that counts.'

'Beer-barrel philosophy,' Holliday said. 'You ready? I'll give us a push.' He hopped down and set his shoulder against the car and got it going.

They stopped in midmorning on a spot of barren prairie, and Skinner pointed to the southeast. 'Fort Elliot's out there, sonny. About three hours off, if you don't sit down too often.'

'Hell, I can't even see it,' Gary said.

'Take a look at your shadow. Keep it there as you walk. By the time the sun moves enough to put you off course, you'll be able to see the post,' Skinner said. 'You feel like shakin', or are you mad at me?'

Gary shook hands with him, then with Holliday, and walked off. When he passed out of earshot, Ben Holliday said, 'You were a little rough on him, Skinner.'

'Got to grow up fast out here, Mr. Holliday. In Texas, a boy's a boy, and a man's a man. One day he ain't ready to shave, and the next day he's got a beard.' He sighed. 'Sure wish I'd got a couple of them cigars off him.' He threw his weight onto the handle, and the car started to move toward the end of track.

60

CHAPTER FOUR

End of track was turning into a tent town surrounded by piles of telegraph poles and boxed equipment, and after Holliday and Skinner wrestled the handcar off the rails, they walked down a ways to where Emil Kisdeen had set up headquarters.

When he saw them he made a surprised face, then took Holliday inside his tent and waved him into a folding chair. Already a line of poles was stretching southwest and the wagons were coming and going regularly; Kisdeen was working three shifts around the clock.

'What's this about you finding some new money?' Kisdeen asked. 'My operator picked up Curly's transmission to Dodge. It caused a flurry of excitement around here.'

Holliday dippered some water from a nearby bucket and slowly poured it over his head. Then he sighed and wiped his face with a handkerchief. 'Let's hope it creates the some flurry in Dodge, enough to give me some credit for more poles and wire.'

'There's nothing to the rumor?' Kisdeen asked.

'Not a damned thing,' Holliday said. He liked Kisdeen, and he trusted him, still he did not mention that there were some buyers interested in the line. Not that he felt it was none of Kisdeen's business, but because he hadn't quite figured out the ramifications of the offer. Without a doubt, someone thought he could make money with the line, and to do that he'd have to operate it.

'It's a bad way to do business,' Kisdeen said softly. 'What makes you think anyone in Dodge will believe it?'

'A hunch,' Holliday said. He got up and went to the flap door and ducked his head to step outside. A fringe-topped buggy was approaching, pulled by a pair of matched roans. The rig wheeled into the camp and stopped in a swelter of dust. A burly, heavy-shouldered man got down and started to walk around the rig to help the woman, but Ben Holliday stepped forward, put his hands on the soft roundness of her waist, and lowered her to the ground.

'Thank you,' she said, smiling with her eyes. She was not tall, and her hair reminded him of polished burl walnut. Her face was round and deeply tanned, and a scatter of freckles tinted the bridge of her nose.

The man said, 'Fella, we help our own women. You understand?'

Emil Kisdeen came out of his tent then and offered his hand to the man. 'Mr. Singer, I'd like to have you meet Mr. Holliday.'

Singer reared a little in surprise. Then he laughed. 'If I'd know that, I wouldn't have spoken so quickly. This is my daughter, Betty.' He plucked two cigars from his pocket and pressed one on Ben Holliday. 'My son, Carl, is standing by on the other end. We can see the poles from our front porch. In another hour the hookup ought to be made and the first message sent. Here, let me give you a light.' He chuckled softly. 'That's the way to get the job done; work day and night until it's finished. And I can assure you, Mr. Holliday, that Lazy T is not ungrateful for this mark of progress.'

Ben Holliday smiled. 'Well that's fine, Mr. Singer. I may have to remind you of what you said in six months or so when we come to acquire a right of way, so you'll be friendly to the idea.'

'Right of way?' Singer said.

'Of course. Did you think end of track would always remain here? Mr. Singer, a railroad has to terminate, yes, but not in the middle of the prairie.' He rolled the cigar from one side of his mouth to the other. 'The railroad takes your cattle north, but it can bring supplies in. And we pay for the right of way, if the price is right.' Then he laughed. 'Well, it's too hot to talk business today anyway.'

'Yes,' Singer said, glad the subject was being dropped. 'We came here to invite Mr. Kisdeen to the ranch for the night. I'd like to extend the invitation to you, Mr. Holliday.'

'I think I'd better stay here,' Kisdeen said.

'After I get a clear signal I want to start putting together some kind of a loading chute.' His glance touched Singer. 'I can expect the cattle to arrive day after tomorrow, can't I.'

'Oh, I think so,' Singer said. 'Yes, yes, I suppose so. But you don't even have any cars here.'

'Mr. Singer, we can get a train here in four hours,' Holliday said. 'Now we're pretty anxious to complete your shipping contract and get on with other business.' He took a hunting case watch from his pocket and glanced at it. 'Don't you think we ought to get started if we're going to reach your place by dark?'

A frown came to Singer's blunt face. 'I thought you wanted to hear the signal when the wires were connected.'

Holliday laughed. 'We're not experimenting with a new invention. It'll work and that's all I care about.' Betty laughed and he looked at her. 'What did I say?'

'It's not what you say, Mr. Holliday, but the way you say it, as though there was one burning desire in you—to run a railroad.'

'I suppose,' Ben said. 'that's about the size of it. Don't you have a burning desire?'

'That's almost an improper question,' Betty Singer said. 'I'll have to think about it.'

'I suppose we'd better go,' Singer said, turning to the buggy. 'But damn it, I did want to hear the wire come alive. There ought to be a celebration or something.' He was still grumbling when he climbed in and Holliday lifted Betty up, then got in back. Ollie Skinner came trotting along the track and when he stopped by the off-wheel he was out of breath. Singer looked at him and said, 'I thought you left the country.' He pointed to Skinner. 'I threw this man off my place once.' His heavy lips mirrored an unyielding opinion of Skinner. 'The man's a thief.'

'He works for me,' Holliday said. 'And I've found him loyal, hard-working, honest, and sober.' He caught Skinner's astonished expression from the corner of his eye, but kept his face straight.

'This man?' Singer yelled, pointing.

'You heard him, didn't you?' Skinner asked. He unbuckled his shell belt, wrapped it around the holstered .44, and handed it to Ben Holliday. 'You just sleep with that tonight; he'll accuse you of anything.'

Anger stained Singer's face. 'Damn you, Skinner, you stole eight dollars from me.'

'Did eight months in the Tascosa jail fer it too!' He stepped back, his wrinkled face bland, the unfriendliness hidden behind drooped eyelids. 'See you, when you get back, Mr. Holliday.'

As Murray Singer drove away, Betty said, 'That dirty old man!' She glanced at Holliday as though she expected him to agree with her, and found that he didn't. 'Don't you believe my father?'

'Sure, but like Skinner said; he's already been in jail.'

Singer turned his attention away from his driving to speak. 'I'll tell you plainly, Holliday, that it lowers my opinion of the railroad to see you're hiring men like that.'

'Probably all your men sing in the choir,' Holliday said casually. 'It's wonderful to be pure.'

Murray Singer said something unintelligible and Betty pouted. She said, 'And I thought I was going to like you, Mr. Holliday.'

The ride turned out to be dusty and silent and very long, and Ben Holliday rather enjoyed it, for he had prodded this stuffed-shirt cattleman on the peck, which wasn't especially hard to do with these Texans, except when it was done for a reason.

And Ben Holliday had a reason.

One long look at Singer, and five minutes of conversation, and Ben knew which way the wind blew. Singer was a big man, with a lot of land and a lot of cattle and two dozen men working for him, and the habit of running things was pretty well ingrained. The telegraph line gave him the notion that now he controlled a little bit of the railroad too. Well, to Ben's way of thinking, he didn't feel any too secure as the boss to begin with, so he had no wish for a dominant man like Singer to even touch the controls.

66

Some men just wouldn't let go once they got hold, and Holliday was certain that Singer was that kind.

Singer had built a sizable place, a large, rambling house with a small-town-size scatter of outbuildings and corrals. He was, Holliday could see, proud of the place, and when he stopped by the porch and got down, he said, 'Out here there's only one thing that holds a man down. Water. Could hardly make a go of it until I got water. Dug four wells to get it, though.'

'Dry holes?' Holliday asked.

'Just a lot of stinkin' wind,' Singer said, turning to the porch.

Holliday handed Betty Singer to the ground; she flounced into the house, and Murray Singer scowled slightly. 'A high-strung girl there. Come on in, Holliday. A whisky would settle some of this dust.'

'Sounds good,' Ben said, and started across the porch. Then he stopped and studied two men walking toward him from the barn. They would have passed on without noticing him if he hadn't said, 'How's your jaw, Satchel?'

They stopped and Satchel looked at him, then did a right face and walked to the porch. His jaw was swollen and discolored clear up to the eye and down into the neck. 'Well, if it ain't the railroad man,' Satchel said. He raised a hand to his face and let it drop away, as though he hadn't meant to do that at all, but couldn't help it. 'Maybe I'll see you before you leave.'

'If you think you have to,' Holliday said. He stood there while the other man pulled Satchel's arm, then Holliday went into the house with Murray Singer.

'Heard about the horse and buggy,' Singer said. 'Satchel doesn't like to be jumped.'

'I had somewhat of a surprise myself,' Holliday said. They went into the parlor, a wide, spacious room filled with Spanish furniture and olla jugs hanging from the beam ceiling. The chandelier was a wagon wheel hung on a chain, with the lamps dangling from hooks set into the rim. 'A beautiful place,' Holliday said. He sat down when Singer made a motion to his hand, then a Mexican servant came in.

'Bring up two whiskies, Ortiz. Then see if you can find my son.' He turned to Holliday. 'Carl is like my right arm, Holliday. Without him, Lazy T would only run half as smooth.'

The servant came back with the whisky and Holliday took his glass, trying to think of an appropriate toast, something about cattle and railroads being wedded, but he had no opportunity to propose it. Singer tossed off his drink, then wiped his watering eyes.

'I suppose you'd like to see the telegraph installation,' Singer said. 'We've put the operator in an old tool shed.' He opened a side door and they walked down a short hall to the side entrance. The tool shed was behind the barn, identified by the string of poles leading to it, and the wire disappearing inside.

While they were crossing the yard, two horsemen rode toward the house. Singer stopped and said, 'Here's Hutchins and Vale. I thought it would be nice if we got together this evening, since we're all in business together.'

Vale was a big man, heading a big outfit, the Cross A. He had a full, florid face and a roan mustache and a pearlhandled pistol at his hip, His handclasp was bone-bruising, and his voice a strong bass. 'Glad to meet you, Holliday. I was beginning to take you for an office man.' He touched Hutchins on the shoulder. 'Bert Hutchins, of the Box X.'

Holliday shook hands with him. Hutchins was like a small rooster, proud standing, bold in the eye, and assertive as only a short man can be.

'We were going to have a look at the telegraph,' Singer said. He laughed. 'Lacking Holliday's confidence, I don't even know if the damned thing works yet.'

They went on together to the tool shed, and Holliday stopped in the open door. The operator was lying on his bunk, and he got up quickly. 'Hello, Mr. Holliday. I guess you caught me loafin'.'

'I don't expect you to stand at attention all the time,' Ben said. 'When did you get through?'

'Some time ago,' the operator said. The key started to chatter, and he listened a moment. 'That's Curly, sir. Want me to take it down? He's calling end of track.'

'Let's find out what's going on,' Singer said. 'That's what he's here for, ain't he?'

'Go ahead,' Holliday said, and the operator wrote the message out. He handed it to Holliday, and Singer crowded in to see and Ben turned to him with a flat, irritated stare. 'Do you mind? This is railroad business.' He read the message and put it in his pocket, then looked at the anger staining Singer's face. 'The cattle train is leaving the yard at sundown.'

'You could have let me read that,' Singer said.

'I could let you put your feet on my office desk, but I won't,' Holliday said. Then he stepped outside and the others turned with him. A horseman cantered to the barn and flung off, and from the way one of the hands rushed out to take the horse, Holliday knew this was Carl Singer. He was dressed in denims and chaps and a wide-brimmed hat, yet as he walked across the yard, Holliday had the distinct feeling that he had seen the man before, but not dressed like that. He let his mind work on it and by the time Carl Singer came up to them, he had it.

'This is my son, Carl,' Singer said.

Holliday observed him while they shook hands. Young, thirty or thirty-one, he was rather handsome, with a square jaw and fierce dark eyes. Holliday said, 'Didn't I see you get off the train in Comanche yesterday morning?'

Carl Singer's eyes changed for the barest instant, becoming alert. Then he smiled. 'Sorry, you must have me mixed up with someone else. I haven't left the ranch for ten days.'

'My mistake,' Holliday said.

'Well, let's go on into the house,' Singer said, his manner jolly. 'Where are you stringing wire to next, Holliday?'

'Who's ready to ship next?' He looked at Hutchins. 'My maintenance foreman is working three shifts, stringing eight to ten miles of wire every day. We could be at your place by Thursday.'

'That sounds good to me,' Hutchins said.

Betty Singer was in the parlor when they stepped into the room. She had changed her dress to something light and white and she gave Ben Holliday her best smile. 'The heat and dust always make me rude, Mr. Holliday. Will you forgive me?' She put her hand on his and let the fingers bite in a little, and in this way she squeezed an answering smile out of him. 'May I call you Ben?'

'I'd like that.'

'Then we'll go sit on the east veranda,' she said. 'It's always nice there close to sundown, and you can see the prairie change hues before growing dark.'

71

Holliday hesitated an instant, then spoke to the men. 'If you gentlemen will excuse me?'

They murmured their assent and he went out with her; she was telling him of some amusing happening and he was giving her a gentleman's polite attention.

After they passed from earshot, Carl Singer swore softly and said, 'God damn it, I didn't think he'd recognize me.'

'Let's go in the study,' Murray Singer said, and led the way; after the door was closed and they'd taken chairs, he let his face draw into a pucker. 'We've got to watch ourselves around him; he's not exactly stupid.' He turned to a liquor cabinet and brought out a bottle and four glasses. 'I'd like to know what kind of a scheme he's hatching with the Indians to keep them from pulling the wires down.' He waved his finger like a baton. 'Make up your mind to it, that here is a man who covers all his bets.'

'Not all of them,' Carl said. 'When I got off the train, the town was still talking about the trouble he had with Satchel. I think you can make him go off half cocked with out much trouble.' He brought out his tobacco and papers and rolled a smoke. His glance went to Hutchins and Vale. 'Like I was telling Dad, Holliday's in a bad spot. His old man has advised him to sell the line.'

'You don't know this,' Murray said quickly. 'Let's stick to what we know.'

'I think it's a sound assumption,' Carl

72

maintained. 'I was in Holly Bristow's Dodge City office when he showed me a letter from Julius Holliday. The old man thinks the offer is sound and so much as said he would advise his son of the same.'

'But that doesn't mean he'll take it,' Jerry Vale said. 'If he was going to sell, he wouldn't be running a train south and putting up wire.'

'We'll have to make him sell,' Murray Singer said. 'But I want the lines up. It was our original agreement when we signed contracts to get as much out of the railroad as we could for the same offer.' He spread his hands. 'I'd rather have the poles set and the wire up than laying in the equipment yard and have to do it ourselves.' He finished his drink and put the glass aside. 'Holliday's got some idea of how he's going to handle the Indians. Oh, I know, the telegraph will put us in touch with the railroad if the Indians start raiding, but the scheme I'm talking about is the one he's cooked up to keep the Comanches away from the wires.' He gnawed his lip a moment. 'If that scheme didn't work, gentlemen, Ben Holliday would go bust in a hurry.'

'I'd like to see the wires stay up,' Bert Hutchins said.

'One way or another, we'll have Indian trouble.'

'You've fought Indians before,' Vale reminded him. 'Can't you do it again?' He laughed without humor. 'Bert, you always want everything for nothing: We've gone along with Murray this far. I'm for following it all the way through.'

Hutchins shrugged and sat back in his chair, having no more to say. Carl refilled his glass and held it for a moment. 'Holliday intends to string more wire than just to our places. We don't want that.'

'He won't,' Murray said flatly. 'If ever a man was over our barrel, Ben Holliday is. He's broke and everyone knows it. And the only revenue he can get right away is the profit on our shipment. How much is that going to amount to?'

'Enough to keep him on his feet,' Hutchins said. 'He's an odds player, a man who will draw to a busted flush and fill it. Hell, it isn't that hard to figure him out. Any revenue he takes in he'll pour into more poles and wire until every rancher within a decent distance will be shipping.' He shook his finger at Murray Singer. 'And that is something we can't control. That's the profit that will make Midland-Pacific stock jump, and our offer worthless.'

'Sure,' Singer said. 'But if the Indians tear down the wire and start raiding, how easy do you think it will be to talk anyone else into the idea?' He shook his head. 'I've never known a man who couldn't be broken, and that sure as hell includes Ben Holliday. So we ship, so he pockets a profit. That's company money, and

74

when we buy the company, we get all the assets, along with the rolling stock and equipment. Once it's ours, God help any Indian who gets in the way.'

The study was filling with evening shadows, and Murray Singer got up, lit several lamps, then poured a little more whisky into his glass. 'I found out today that Ollie Skinner is working for the railroad.'

'Hell, I knew that,' Carl said. 'He's been working for them since he got out of jail.'

'You never said anything to me,' Murray said.

Carl shrugged. 'Now how important did you think it was? Hell, after you had Skinner locked up, you said you never wanted to see him again. That's why I didn't say anything.'

'Skinner's worked his way into Holliday's good graces,' Murray said. 'So I'll assume that Skinner knows some things we ought to know.'

'Could be,' Carl said. 'So?'

'Since Skinner would never come here, better take Satchel with you and ride to end of line. Maybe you can get Skinner alone.'

Carl Singer laughed. 'What the hell do you think Skinner will tell me? Except to go to hell.'

'Don't you know how to get what you want from a man?' Vale asked.

Carl Singer frowned. 'You want it that way, Dad? Skinner is tough. He'll have to be hurt.'

'We're talking about a hundred-thousand

dollar investment,' Bert Hutchins said flatly. 'Who the devil cares who gets hurt?'

A soft run of talk came from the hall, then Betty Singer laughed at something Holliday said, and knocked on the study door. She opened it and pouted prettily. 'You're like hermits. It's a beautiful sunset,' she said, and sat down. 'I've been trying to talk Ben into staying a few days, but he's very stubborn. I think he's dedicated to working himself to death before he's thirty-five.'

'Never knock an ambitious man,' Vale said, smiling. 'Sit down, Holliday. Care for a drink?'

'Too close to supper,' Ben said. 'But I'll sit.' He let a smile build slowly. 'However, with such a beautiful daughter, Mr. Singer, I was sorely tempted to let the railroad go to pot for a few days.'

'Things have a way of taking care of themselves.' Hutchins opined. 'When I was thirty and running four hundred head, I wouldn't leave the place if one of my cows was ready to drop a calf. Now I let it happen and count heads every spring and fall.'

'Unfortunately,' Holliday said, 'when I need a new boxcar, I can't expect the caboose to give birth to it. I have to buy it with hard cash, and there is a shortage of that at the present which I hope to remedy,' He turned his head as the servant quietly entered.

'A man to see Señor Holliday, *jefe.*'

'Send him in,' Murray Singer said. He

looked at Ben Holliday. 'Were you expecting anyone?'

'No,' Holliday said, genuinely puzzled. He waited and then he heard hard boots coming down the hall. When Ollie Skinner stopped in the doorway, Ben said, 'Don't you believe in the telegraph?'

'Got to talk to you,' Skinner said.

'Excuse me,' Holliday said, and stepped out of the room. But this didn't satisfy Skinner, who took him out of the house, out to where his horse was waiting. Ben said, 'What the hell's the matter with you, Skinner?'

'Bender came back,' Skinner said. 'He's waitin' fer you at end of line.'

'Why didn't you telegraph it and save the ride?'

Skinner wiped his face. 'I don't want anyone to know but you, Mr. Holliday. Me, I don't trust nothin' here, or nobody. You know, I never took that eight dollars like Singer said. But I did a stretch in jail for it.' He glanced past Holliday to the house. 'A man does me mean once, and I got no use for him from then on. Maybe you'd better borrow a horse. I'll wait and ride back with you.'

Holliday nodded and went back into the house, thinking how easy it would be to tell Skinner he was imagining things. But Holliday wasn't going to dismiss the man's opinion that casually, especially when Carl Singer said he hadn't left the ranch, while he'd gotten off the train in Comanche. A man had a reason to lie, maybe a personal one, but Holliday would be better off, he knew, if he didn't let any of the Singers get too friendly until he knew more about this.

He made his excuses, the best in the world; business, and Murray Singer made a fuss about being sorry this had come up, but he didn't argue about it. Holliday said good-bye to Betty, and promised he'd see her again, then went out with Murray and Carl.

Skinner was still waiting by his horse, and Carl went to the barn to fetch one for Ben Holliday. Murray said, 'It's a long ride on an empty stomach, Holliday. Are you sure you couldn't—'

'Skinner says it's important.'

Singer shrugged. 'You're the best judge of that. But it's still a shame you both have to ride hungry. Skinner, why don't you stay and eat before going back?'

'I guess not,' the old man, said sourly.

'Now you're not letting bitter feelings stand in the way of a full belly, are you?' Singer laughed softly. 'Can't a man show that he was wrong and sorry about it?' Carl came back with a saddle horse, and Murray Singer said, 'I've just asked Skinner to stay for supper, but he won't accept my apologies.'

'You never were very good at it,' Carl said. 'Ollie, we found out that someone else took that eight dollars. None of us knew how to tell

78

you, knowing how yon felt about us and all.' He scuffed dust with his feet. 'Hell, man, you can hold it against us forever. Have supper, anyway.'

'Nope,' Skinner said bluntly, stubbornly.

Murray was beginning to lose patience, but Carl stayed amiable. 'We said we were sorry. What more do you want?'

'Who took the money?' Skinner asked.

'The one they called Rio,' Carl said. 'You remember him. He told us he took it.'

'That's right,' Murray said, backing his son up. 'Rio said he took the money.'

Skinner squeezed tobacco juice between his lips and stepped into the saddle. He sat there and looked at the Singers. 'I always said you was liars, and I'll still say it. Rio never took the money. I did. He owed it to me from poker and wouldn't pay up.' He grinned. 'You want to try another story?

Carl Singer swore and took a step toward the old man, but Murray flung out his arm, blocking him. 'All right, get out of here, Skinner. The next time I see you on my place, you won't ride off.'

'Suits me,' Skinner said, and turned his horse, but Ben Holliday did not.

'When I first met you, Carl, I mentioned that I'd seen you get off the train in Comanche. And I did, in spite of what you said. Now you come up with this story. Playing games, gentlemen?'

'It's our business,' Murray Singer said. 'Leave it that way.'

'We'll see,' Holliday said, and joined Skinner; they trotted away together. When they were out of the yard, Ben said, 'Now you tell the straight of it. Did you or didn't you take the money?'

'Told you once I didn't. Rio didn't either. He couldn't have, because he'd been loaned to Vale on roundup.' He checkled softly. 'That's why I confessed that I took it; they was ready to believe that. It sure threw 'em, didn't it?'

'But not hard,' Holliday said. 'This is a high-stake game, Ollie, and the pot is a railroad.' He thought about it a moment. 'And it makes me wonder if Hutchins and Vale are counting chips.'

'Think you dare chance that they ain't?' Skinner asked. He turned and looked back at the Singer ranch, bright with lights. 'Was a man to come ridin' across the prairie at night and see that, he'd think it was the friendliest sight he'd ever seen. Shows how wrong a man can be without even tryin'.'

CHAPTER FIVE

Jim Bender was in the cook tent when Holliday pushed the flap aside and stepped in. Bender sat with his hands enclosing a cup of coffee, and Holliday poured some for himself before sitting down. The cook was washing the last of the supper dishes and he set a pan of stew on the back of the stove to warm for Holliday and Skinner, who was putting up the horses.

'I thought you were hunting Indians,' Holliday said.

'I was,' Bender said. 'That's why I went to Fort Elliot, who makes a business of keeping track of the Indians.' He grinned and rubbed his beard stubble. 'A man can save a lot of riding that way.' He grinned at Ben Holliday. 'I didn't expect to find you out here at end of track. I was going to telegraph you, but Skinner said you were with the Singers.'

'You know them well?'

Bender shrugged. 'Well enough. Murray likes to get what he wants, and the best way to stay clear of him is never to have what he wants.' He leaned back and rolled a cigarette. 'While I was at Fort Elliot, a new lieutenant wandered in off the prairie. Created somewhat of a stir; they usually don't arrive that way. As it happened, I was in Dawson's office when he reported. He said you were going to string wire to the post. Naturally I was some surprised.'

'If I can get wire and poles,' Holliday said. 'What did Dawson say about the telegraph?'

'He'd like to believe it,' Bender said. 'Fact is, he'll be here in the mornin' to talk it over, among other things.'

'What other things?'

'I don't know,' Bender admitted. 'He don't take me into his confidence.' He got up to refill his coffee cup, then Skinner came in and headed for the stove and the pot of stew there. 'Now there's a suspicious old man, Ben.' There was more praise in Bender's voice than condemnation. 'If you want to know about the Singers, ask Skinner. It'll be bad, because he never saw anything good in any of 'em, and it'll be the truth.

'Who do I see to get the other side?'

Bender thought a minute. 'Holly Bristow. He used to have a law office in Comanche, but he moved to Dodge four years ago.'

'Now that's real interesting,' Holliday said, thinking of his father's letter and the offer from the Dodge City lawyer.

'What's real interestin'?' Skinner asked, bringing his plate to the table.

'Holly Bristow,' Holliday said. 'I just found out he was thick with Murray Singer.'

'That crook,' Skinner said, and began eating. Bender glanced at Holliday and shrugged, then got up.

82

'There's no sense in me hanging around, Ben. According to Dawson, the Indians are somewhere to the north, huntin' buffalo. Maybe I'll see you in a week or ten days.' He pushed Skinner's hat down over his eyes. 'Didn't anyone ever tell you to take your hat off when you eat?'

After he walked out, Skinner said, 'There was a time when Jim and Betty Singer was talkin' about settin' up housekeepin'. Thought I'd mention that for what it's worth.'

'Just what is it worth?' Holliday asked.

'Wouldn't know,' Skinner said. 'Maybe you'd better ask him sometime.'

Holliday went out and stood in the darkness for a time, then walked over to the tent Emil Kisdeen had left behind. The maintenance superintendent had taken the work trail a ways north, where the night shift, working by lantern light, were setting poles for the line to Bert Hutchins' place. As he took off his boots, Holliday wondered what kind of a reply Harry Lovell got from the Western Union stockyard in Dodge concerning the poles and wire. There was no particular good will between Midland-Pacific and Western Union, since the railroad had already cost the telegraph company considerable money. The wire and poles from Dodge to Comanche had been put in by Western Union, for the railroad, but when bad turned to worse, Western Union sold it to Midland-Pacific at a loss, expecting the railroad to go broke so they could buy it back and break even. But the railroad was stubborn and kept hanging on, and now they were asking for more credit.

He was thinking about his dismal prospects when he fell asleep.

Carl Singer dismounted a hundred yards from the tents and squatted for a time. Satchel remained on his horse, his hands crossed on the pommel. Finally Singer said, 'You'd better go in alone; he'd spook if he saw me.'

'He's no friend of mine,' Satchel said. 'What makes you think—'

'Just get him away from the camp. I'll foot in and wait for you.'

'How'll I know where he's sleepin'?'

'It won't be in a tent,' Carl Singer said. 'Look on the ground around the edge of camp.' He gave the man a shove. 'Get going and don't wake everyone up.' He watched Satchel disappear in the darkness, then moved in closer.

Every tent was dark, and there was no one about when Satchel soft-footed it around the camp. He found Skinner sleeping on a tie pile, and eased his revolver clear of the holster before moving in too close.

Carefully, Satchel advanced until he could hear Skinner breathe, then he pressed the cold muzzle of the pistol against Skinner's temple. 'One sound,' Satchel said, 'and I'll blow you to kingdom come.'

Without moving his head, Skinner opened his eyes with a snap, rolled them, and saw Satchel standing there.

'Up,' Satchel said softly. 'Come on, up!' Without taking the pistol away from Skinner's head, the man patted around, trying to find Skinner's gun.

'I gave it to Holliday,' Skinner said. 'You want to do the smart thing, Satchel? Take that pistol away from my head and vanish. If you don't, I swear, I'll even this with you.'

'Let's go,' Satchel said. 'We'll go or I'll scatter your brains now.'

'You got a good argument there,' Skinner said, and jumped down off the tie pile. The pistol prodding him in the back directed him past the camp, then he saw Carl Singer standing there in the darkness. 'I might have known it,' he said gruffly. 'Was you scared to come in fer me yourself?'

'Go catch up his horse, Satchel,' Singer said. 'I'll keep Ollie company.'

'Some company,' Skinner grumbled. He waited in silence for a time, then turned to Singer. 'If this is your notion, it ain't a good one.'

'I only want to talk to you,' Singer said. 'Ollie, you're a hard man to get along with.'

'Haven't heard any complaints,' Skinner said. Satchel came back with a horse, and Carl Singer motioned for him to mount up. When Skinner showed some reluctance, Singer hit

85

him with the gun barrel, not hard enough to knock him out, but hard enough to hurt him.

'I'm not going to fool with you,' Singer said, and got on his own horse. They rode out with Ollie Skinner between them, and kept up a steady pace for over an hour.

Their destination was a dry wash, a ten-foot-deep gully splitting the face of the prairie in an irregular line. Satchel took care of the horses and Carl Singer crouched down, his gun still covering Skinner.

'We can talk here,' Singer said. 'I'll ask questions, and you'll answer 'em, Ollie.'

'If I know the answers,' Skinner said.

'Oh, you're a smart old bastard,' Carl said. 'You know a lot, say a lot.' He turned his head as Satchel came back. 'Fix a fire. I saw some brush along here earlier today.' Satchel stomped around, breaking up brush, and finally got a small fire going. Then he sat down and pointed his gun at Ollie Skinner. 'I'll keep an eye on him, Mr. Singer.'

'Be careful, he's sneaky as hell,' Carl said. He took a cigar from his pocket and lit it. 'I'll save you the butt, Ollie. You always used to pick up snipes for chewing tobacco.' He laughed. 'When I put my mind to it, there's a lot of things about you I don't like.'

'Same here,' Skinner said, 'only I don't have to put my mind to it.'

'Let's get on with this,' Satchel said. 'I want to get out of here by daylight.'

'You're right,' Carl said. 'We want to talk over some railroad business, Ollie.'

'I fetch meals, tend horses, and run errands,' Skinner said. 'What do I know?'

'You've got your ear to every keyhole, Ollie. I figure you know what's goin' on. Is Holliday going to take the offer made to him?'

'What offer?'

Satchel hit him with a heavy stick and Skinner fell over. But he sat up again, a red welt on the side of his head. Carl Singer spoke. 'A lawyer in Dodge made an offer to buy the line. Is Holliday going to take it?'

'Ask Holliday. He's the boss.'

Again Satchel struck him with the club, across the mouth, and Skinner bled from the lips. He sat up more slowly this time and spat out a broken tooth. Carl said, 'What do you want to be like that for, Ollie? You cooperate, and I'll give you a horse and fifty dollars.' He looked at Skinner to see how the offer was goin to be taken, but there was nothing in the old man's expression except disgust. 'All right, we've got some time. How does Holliday expect to keep the Indians from tearing down the telegraph wires?'

'Are they goin' to tear down the wires? I didn't hear nobody say that.'

Satchel would have hit him again, but Carl blocked his arm. 'He's not afraid of that club, Satchel. Ollie, we don't want to hurt you, but we want to know about these things. The

87

Indians will sure as hell tear the wires down once they find out what they're for. Now what's Holliday goin' to do about it?'

'Pray,' Skinner said. 'Write to his congressman. How the hell do I know?'

'You know,' Carl said. He looked at Satchel. 'We've been too easy on Ollie. Strip him to the waist.'

The man-got up and started for Skinner, but made the mistake of putting his pistol into the holster first. It was all the break Skinner needed; he kicked Satchel flush in the face and drove him backwards full into the fire. Satchel lit in a sitting position, his tight denims no protection at all. With a scream he vaulted up and started rolling away, and Skinner dived for Carl Singer.

For a moment they just rolled on the ground, their arms locked tightly about each other, legs thrashing for purchase; then Skinner battered Singer's face with his knuckles and tried to break away, to climb the gully wall.

He almost made the top when Singer pulled his gun, sighted quickly, and smashed Ollie Skinner's hip. The old man cried out and tumbled down, then Singer got up and went over and stood there, looking at him.

'I could have killed you easy,' Carl said.

'You'd have-saved time if-you had,' Skinner said, panting.

'Satchel, quit that moaning and strip him

88

like I said!'

Skinner was shorn of shirt, and his underwear was ripped clean to the waist, then Satchel went to his saddlebags and brought back four picket pins and some short lengths of rope. In spite of his wound, Skinner fought, and it took both of them to spread-eagle him.

After Skinner's arms and legs were both tied tightly, Carl sat back and wiped sweat from his face. 'Ollie, you're making me do this.'

'I ain't makin' you do nothin',' Skinner snapped. 'It's your own damned meanness.'

'Put a little fire on his belly,' Singer said.

Skinner drew taut like a violin string when Satchel laid a burning twig on him, and he moaned and bit his lips and sawed his head from side to side until Singer couldn't stand it any longer.

'Get it off him,' Carl said, and Satchel flicked the burning wood away. 'Ollie, I've got to know about Holliday's plans. What's he to you, anyway? It's just a job, ain't it?'

'You wouldn't understand,' Skinner said softly. 'He only cusses me when I got it comin', not when he feels like it. Burn me if you want. That's all I'm going to say.'

Carl Singer didn't believe that, so they put some more fire on Skinner, and after a while, when he lost consciousness, Singer realized that it was the truth; Skinner just wasn't going to speak again.

'I should have known him better,' Singer said softly. 'He was never known to back down on anythin' in his life.' He got up and brushed off the seat of his pants. 'Let's go.'

'He'll talk if we leave him,' Satchel said.

'No. You get the horses.' When Satchel turned, Carl Singer drew his gun and cocked it. 'Damn you, Ollie, you're the world's worst fool.' He fired and then cocked the gun and shot two more times, because he was a little frightened now and doubted his own ability to kill this old man. Then he turned and walked down the gully to where Satchel waited with the horses. 'Leave Skinner's horse here.' He stepped into the saddle, but Satchel remained dismounted. 'Well, you want to stay here with him?'

'I can't ride,' Satchel said. 'My butt's one big blister.'

'Then walk,' Carl Singer said harshly. 'You'll make it all right.'

'I don't want to be found anywhere around here,' Satchel said flatly.

'Who the hell's going to find you?' Singer asked. 'If he's missed, it won't be until daylight. And who the hell cares enough about him to go looking for him?'

'Holliday.'

'He's a greenhorn who has a hell of a time finding his way from the house to the barn.' He gigged his horse and ran up the steep walls of the gully, and once clear, he set a brisk pace

90

back to his father's place. He wasn't sorry he had killed Ollie Skinner; he was bothered more by the possible consequences of what he had done; he'd hang for it if he was caught, and this seemed grossly unfair to Carl, hanging for killing a worthless old coot like Skinner.

Murray Singer was still up when Carl rode in. The house was dark, save for a lamp on in the parlor, and Murray came out to the porch as his son dismounted.

'Well?'

Carl shook his head and sat on the steps. 'He wouldn't talk.'

Murray Singer took the cigar from his mouth. 'What the hell do you mean, he didn't talk? Can't you get information out of a man?'

'Not him,' Carl said. 'Satchel and I put fire to him, but he still wouldn't say. Maybe if he'd hated me less, he'd have been less stubborn.'

'Where's Satchel?' Murray asked, peering around in the darkness.

'Walking. Skinner put up a fight. Knocked Satchel in the fire and he burned his hind end.'

'Why, you damned bunglers,' Murray said softly. 'Where's Skinner now?'

'In a dry wash. Dead.'

'Well, at least you had enough sense to do that,' Murray said. 'You didn't leave anything behind to point to you, did you? Like some empty shells or something?'

'No, I've still got the empties in my gun,' Carl said.

'Well, go in and clean it and put it away. Start carrying another from now on. There's no telling when Jim Bender will come snooping around.'

'If he does,' Carl said, 'Betty can handle him.'

'Like the last time?' Murray shook his head. 'He surprised the hell out of me, thinking more of that damned badge than he did Betty. You clean the gun and put it away someplace. I want everyone to be lily white when Bender shows up.'

The cavalry arrived shortly after dawn, a ten-man escort for the colonel. Holliday was having his breakfast when they pulled into camp and he told the cook to set out some more plates in a hurry; it wouldn't hurt to feed the cavalry for the sake of public relations.

Colonel Cameron Dawson was a tall, gaunt man with a roan mustache and a constantly worried air. He shook hands briefly, then sat down and ignited a cigar. The fact that the cook was setting a place for his line troopers pleased Dawson, and he gave orders for the sergeant to see that every man was washed before he came in.

With some coffee before him, Dawson's manner thawed somewhat. 'Mr. Holliday, since your response to my written appeals could hardly be classified as encouraging, it's come as considerable surprise to me that your attitude has been reversed.'

'Blame it on a bright lieutenant,' Holliday said.

Dawson's eyebrow arched. 'Mr. Gary? He is now working off a bit of stable detail for arriving late. Now about the telegraph line to Fort Elliot. Fact or fiction?'

'Fact, if I can promote the poles and wire from Western Union.'

'The eternal catch,' Dawson said sadly. 'I was afraid something like this was going to happen.'

'There's about a seventy-thirty chance,' Ben pointed out. 'That's better than before, isn't it?'

'Good reasoning, but which is it? Seventy against getting the poles, or for?'

'Against,' Holliday said frankly. 'Our credit is none too good. However, I hope to convince others that it will improve.'

'You're a gambler,' Dawson said. 'And they make me nervous. Always gambling with something not entirely theirs.' Then he shrugged. 'But this telegraph is going to cost me. How much?'

'No more than you're used to paying,' Ben said. 'Colonel, I've got to move beef and freight over the line or go broke. And to do that, I have to assure the Texans that when there's Indian trouble, the railroad will do its fair share in putting it down. Naturally I'm going to pass as much of this off to the army as I can, and so they can do a good job of it I'll put in a telegraph.' He smiled. 'I think you're clever enough to see that when it comes to whether the Indians go or the railroad does, it'll be the Indians. So we end up making deals with each other. For taking care of the Indians, you'll get a supply line moved a lot nearer, and communication with Fort Dodge. Progress, Colonel, is a complicated thing.'

Cameron Dawson thought about it, then nodded. 'And I can see why you held out. No profit in it for you.'

'Exactly. You'd have done the same.' The troopers came in and sat down, and the cook brought out platters of hot cakes and bacon. 'Cookie, when you're through there, go out and find Skinner. I've got a job for him.'

'Sure, Mr. Holliday.'

Holliday gave his attention then to the colonel. 'Jim Bender, who's working for me now, is going to arrange a meeting with the Indians. We're going to demonstrate to them how dangerous it will be to tamper with the telegraph wires.'

'How? Shoot the first one that touches it?'

Holliday laughed and shook his head. He then explained his plan to Colonel Dawson, and Dawson was pleased with it, although sparing in his praise. 'It would be a good thing, Colonel, if you were present at the demonstration. It's my opinion that this ought to be carried out with considerable pomp and ceremony. I hope I can count on you, Colonel,

94

for some original thoughts.'

Dawson laughed. 'Mr. Holliday, God help us if you run for the United States Senate. Yes, I think I can add some touches.' He turned his head and spoke to a sergeant sitting at the third mess table. 'DuJoise!'

He was a small peppery man with a waxed mustache and a manner of clicking his heels together that suggested foreign service, and a lot of it. Dawson introduced him. 'Mr. Holliday, this is Sergeant Jean Jacques DuJoise, late of the French Artillery, the Prussian Royal Lancers, and the Confederate States Army. We call him John-Jack for short, and it's my eternal regret that he isn't a captain.' He motioned for DuJoise to sit down, and he explained Holliday's plan. The Frenchman's eyes brightened and he smiled widely. 'Since you've mastered the Comanche language, John-Jack, I suggest that you consider yourself attached to Mr. Holliday until recalled by me.'

'As you wish,' DuJoise said. 'I'll be delighted to work with you, m'sieu. And we certainly can put on a show for the Comanches.'

'John-Jack had a long and satisfying relationship with a Comanche girl,' Dawson explained. 'If anyone knows their customs better than he does, I've yet to meet him.' He slapped Sergeant DuJoise on the shoulder and got up to have his coffee cup refilled and fetch back a plate of bacon and hot cakes. 'The

95

Indians are on a hunt; I told Bender that yesterday morning. But when the hunt is over, they're going to mix paint and dance some. When's your first load of cattle moving north?'

'I expect a train through today,' Holliday said. 'Probably two days before we're ready to pull out. Why?'

'I was just trying to get your schedule so I could activate a few more patrols,' Dawson said. 'The Indians are getting the idea finally that they can't lick the army, and they hesitate to cut up when patrols are roaming about.'

The cook came back into the tent and approached the table. 'Mr. Holliday, I can't find Skinner anyplace. His horse is here, but there's another one missing, the one you brought back from the Singer place.'

'That's odd,' Ben said. 'Did you have a look around the tie pile? Skinner likes to roost there.'

'Yes, sir, but he ain't there. But his blankets are, though.'

Holliday got up from the table, a frown on his face. 'I think I'll have a look for myself. If you'll excuse me?'

'We'll join you, if you don't mind,' Dawson said. 'John-Jack is pretty good at reading stories from tracks.'

They walked together to the tie pile, but before they got to it, John-Jack stopped. 'A question, m'sieu. Does anyone here wear the boots of the cowboy? With the little heels?'

'Hell no,' Holliday said. 'Mostly work boots around here. Flat heels.' Then he amended that statement. 'Except Skinner.'

DuJoise pointed to the soft earth. 'There to see is another man's boot marks.' He puffed his cheek and thumped it. 'Ah, we follow them to the tie pile, so!' He walked bent over, examining the ground. 'Hah! Two pair of tracks walk away, in that direction.' He pointed south to the flat stretch of prairie.

'Skinner had no reason to leave camp,' Ben Holliday said. 'I don't understand it.'

'Nor do I, m'sieu,' DuJoise said. 'But it would be worth a ride to find out.' He shrugged. 'There is the missing horse also.'

'Skinner had his own horse,' Holliday said. 'He wouldn't take the one belonging to Murray Singer. He hated Singer.' Then he fell silent a moment. 'Could it be that someone got the horse for him?'

'A logical thought,' Dawson said. 'Well, I've got an army to run. If you and John-Jack want to follow this up, go ahead.' He shook hands with Ben Holliday. 'I enjoyed the bargaining, but I'm not sure what kind of cards I held.' He smiled and walked back to the cook tent.

'I'm going to get my gun,' Holliday said. 'I'll meet you here in ten minutes.'

He was going to take the rifle, then picked up Skinner's .44 instead and buckled the belt around his waist. He caught up Skinner's horse, saddled him, and joined the sergeant,

97

who was already mounted.

With DuJoise slightly in the lead, they moved away from camp, taking wide arcs and finally finding the place where Carl Singer had waited.

DuJoise held up three fingers, then they cut to the southeast, moving at a walk, following a trail so faint that Holliday continually lost it, and relied on DuJoise to pick it up. The Frenchman had a profound knowledge of the land, and he read accurately the slightest sign, and watching him work, Holliday could understand in part why so many of the early explorers were French; they seemed temperamentally suited to this exciting work.

Holliday could not imagine why the two men who took Skinner left such a trail. Then he tried to reason it from their point of view and decided that they figured no one in the railroad camp could find a washtub with both hands, so it didn't matter how much of a trail they left.

This made him smile, this mistaken impression, for many times in his own life he had been tripped up by the unexpected, the uncounted happening. Who could have known the army would show up, and that a good tracker would be available?

It was a sobering reminder to Ben Holliday that a man's plans were often thrown into a cocked hat by new elements he hadn't even considered. He promised himself he'd be careful with his own affairs.

They found the dry wash and Ollie Skinner. The flies were gathering and the sun wasn't helping much either. Holliday thought he was going to be sick, but he fought it down. DuJoise brought from his pack a small shovel and Holliday dug the grave while the Frenchman had his look around.

'Not Indians,' DuJoise said softly. 'No, m'sieu, the cowboys do this to your friend. An Indian does not put on fire that way. Just little pieces for the slow pain. And to shoot the victim three times; it is a waste of bullets, and the Indian has none to waste. He would have used a war club.' He stood there, shaking his head. 'And the pins, they are what the cowboys use to tie their horses.' He pointed to the scars on the bank, where they had come down, and where one mounted man had gone up. 'The other was not riding his horse, but leading him.' He came over and spelled Holliday with the digging. 'What is your wish, m'sieu? Return to the camp, or go on?'

'We'll go on,' Holliday said grimly. 'If we can catch the two who did this, I'm going to see they hang for it.'

DuJoise glanced at him. 'And if they choose to fight?'

'Then I'll save the state of Texas the price of a hanging.'

CHAPTER SIX

As soon as Harry Lovell got off the train in Dodge City, he walked along Front Street to Holly Bristow's office, which was over a saddle maker's shop. He used the side stairs, not particularly worried about anyone seeing him, because he didn't come to Dodge often enough to be well known. And Lovell always conducted his business quietly, so as not to attract attention to himself.

A man had to do things that way when he held down three jobs at one time.

Bristow wasn't in his office, so Lovell made himself comfortable and waited, and in time Bristow came back, a fleeting look of surprise on his face when he saw Harry Lovell there.

'I wasn't expecting you,' Bristow said, sitting down. He was a large, round man with a moon face and a dense black mustache. His suit was expensive, and a diamond stickpin in his tie reflected sunlight. 'Have you sent your report to Julius Holliday yet?'

'No,' Lovell said. 'I may skip this one.'

Holly Bristow laughed softly. 'Lovell, you must be getting rich, drawing a salary from the railroad, and a bonus from the old man for checking up on the boy, and from me a generous fee for getting us in on the inside track. How's Holliday coming along?'

'He's trying desperately to save the line,' Lovell said. 'I came to Dodge to get some credit from Western Union. For poles and wire. He wants to string a telegraph to Fort Elliot.'

'I don't like the sound of that,' Bristow said softly. 'There's been a strong rumor going around that Midland-Pacific got some financial help. Any truth to it?'

'None,' Lovell said. 'Holliday started that himself in order to bolster his credit with Western Union.'

'The last time I talked to Carl Singer, he expressed an impatience at the way this is dragging out. Holliday's old man is for taking the offer. What makes Ben so stubborn?'

Lovell shrugged, then said, 'Maybe he doesn't like to be licked, Holly. I can't blame him for that. What am I going to do about the poles and wire? I've got to try, and suppose I get them?'

'Don't do a thing until tomorrow morning,' Bristow said. 'That will give me time to spike your chances. Then you can report back to Ben Holliday with a straight face. Harry, how long is it going to be before his back breaks?'

'I'll be damned if I know,' Lovell admitted. 'He should be bleeding, but he isn't. The sooner this comes to a head, the better off we'll all be.'

'Right,' Bristow said. 'That's what Carl Singer said. Some men have a habit of hanging on and hanging on. We don't want this to happen. Singer made it pretty plain that in a week or so he expects Holliday to throw up his hands and quit. Now if he's not going to do that, it's up to us to put the pressure on him hard.'

'No rough stuff,' Lovell cautioned.

Bristow laughed and waved his hand. 'This is a business venture, Harry, not a war. Cut off his credit here and there, and he's done.' He shuffled a few papers around on his desk. 'We both know that more people have been stabbed to death with a bookkeeper's pencil than the sword. Now I want you to go over to the hotel, get a room, shave, clean up, have a good meal, and talk to anyone who wants to listen. Talk about railroading, Harry, and lay it on the line that Holliday is broke. You know what I mean. Loosen up with the inside information, like a man will when he can't see the sense of keeping quiet when the outfit is staggering its last steps. I'll take it from there, and when you ask for poles and wire, you can bet you won't get them.'

'All right,' Lovell said. Then he sighed. 'God, I wish it would end, Holly. But I've said that before, haven't I? What takes a piddlin' little railroad so long to die?'

'The man at the throttle,' Bristow said. 'Holliday's got his hand on it and he doesn't want to turn loose of it.' He straightened in his chair. 'Be patient, Harry. Remember, we can

102

afford to be.'

'Of course,' Lovell said.

Bristow got up when someone knocked at the door, and Harry Lovell straightened apprehensively, but Bristow motioned for him to sit back and relax. He opened the door and said, 'Yes?' He glanced at the girl, and at the heavy man with the walrus mustache. 'Could I help you?'

'I'm Anna Neubauer. This is my father. May we come in?'

Bristow stepped aside. 'Of course. I was just finishing with a client.' He turned to Harry Lovell. 'I'm sure we'll find your wife, sir. You'll hear from me shortly.' Then he shook hands with Lovell, who went right out. 'Now, Miss Neubauer. Sit down, please. Right over there, sir, in the leather chair.' Again he moved behind his desk and sat down. 'Well, what can I do for you?'

'My father's English is not too good,' Anna said. 'But we want to know if it's true that in America, if you make a new thing, you can take out a paper to keep others from making it too.'

'A patent,' Bristow said, smiling. 'Mr. Neubauer, have you an invention?'

Fritz Neubauer looked confused. *'Was sagt er?'*

Anna explained it in German, and he nodded. *'Ja*, I make this for the train.' He got up. 'I leave it in the hall.' Then he hurried out and came back with a long, shallow box. He put this on Bristow's desk and took off the lid. A model of a railroad-car coupling handcrafted, with two complete sets of trunks, with air brakes, all operated by mechanical linkage made a polished steel and brass display on piano-finished mahogany. 'My daughter, she vill tell you about it. My English—' He shrugged and smiled as though embarrassed.

'This lever here represents the engineer's brake control,' Anna said, demonstrating it. 'The train is stopped when this valve is moved. But there have been many instances where the engineer and fireman were dead, or too badly hurt to operate the control, and the train ran on until an accident happened.'

'Yes, I'm well aware of that,' Bristow admitted. 'Just last year there was a crash out of Sioux Falls—but go on.'

'This is where the engineer stands,' she said. 'And this is a spring-loaded switch. The engineer puts his foot on it all the time he is running the train. If he so much as takes his foot off, the valve will automatically operate the brakes and stop the train.'

'By golly,' Bristow said, 'that sounds very good.' He drew pen and paper to him. 'Now, we have some work to do. First, a complete description of the invention, its parts, and function.' He smiled at Fritz Neubauer. 'Smoke if you like. This is going to take some time.'

After they registered at the hotel, Anna
Neubauer understood how great was her
father's thirst for a glass of beer, and urged
him to go get one, but not to be late for
supper; this was a strange town and she didn't
want to eat alone.

She went upstairs and along the hall to her
room, and as she unlocked the door, Harry
Lovell stepped out of a room a few doors
down. He glanced at her in passing and smiled
fleetingly.

Anna said, 'I hope you find your wife, sir.'

Lovell stopped and frowned. 'What was
that?'

'I said that I hoped the lawyer finds your
wife.'

His recognition of her was complete then,
and he nodded curtly and went on down the
stairs. Just before he disappeared from view he
turned his head and looked at her. Anna
Neubauer shrugged and went into her room.

She knew her father would stay a while in
the saloon, so she washed her face, then went
to do some shopping. Her purchases were
carefully made—she was a born bargainer—
then she walked back to the hotel just as her
father crossed the street. He had, she knew,
not limited himself to one beer, but three, but
she expected this. Had she said three, he

105

would have had five or six, for he was that way in some things, as though he sought to show in small harmless ways his independence from domesticity.

They ate in the dining room, and Fritz Neubauer seemed troubled, and finally he came out with it, speaking softly in German. 'I've seen that man before, Anna.'

'What man?'

'The one in the lawyer's office. I think he works for the railroad.'

She shrugged. 'So? We work for the railroad and we went there.'

'I'm sure he works for the railroad. Not with the hands. For Mr. Holliday, in the office building.' He shook his head and went on eating. 'Maybe he invents something, yes?'

'He is trying to find his wife, Papa.'

'How could a man lose his wife?' He seemed to think this was the most ridiculous thing he ever heard.

*　　*　　*

Through the heat of the day, Ben Holliday and John-Jack DuJoise followed the trail across the prairie, feeling it grow hotter with each mile. Finally DuJoise prodded some horse droppings. 'No more than an hour, m'sieu. Perhaps even less. But no more.' He pulled his hat low over his eyes and squinted at the shimmering reaches of land. 'He still walks his

106 .

horse, and at a slow pace. See how close are the marks of his feet.' He paused to think a moment, then added, 'I don't think he limps, m'sieu. Still it is not the stride of a well man. The feet are held too far apart.' He turned to his horse. 'Come. We move faster now.'

Now and then they trotted their horses, and in the distance Ben Holliday could make out the buildings of the Singer place, and as far as he was concerned, this pretty well settled the issue, for if it wasn't a Singer man who killed Skinner, then it was someone who felt pretty safe on Singer property.

As they drew close to the yard, they split, John-Jack going on toward the corral and bunkhouse, and Ben Holliday riding toward the front porch. Carl and Murray Singer came out to stand.

Holliday did not bother to dismount. He said, 'Mr. Singer, Ollie Skinner is dead. The man that killed him is here, on your place. I want him.'

For a moment, Murray Singer said nothing, then he smiled. 'Son, I can't say that I know a Texas Ranger who'd have enough nerve to do what you just did. In Texas, we're a little more careful about what we say.' He turned his head and looked at John-Jack DuJoise. 'What the hell's that soldier doin' snoopin' around my corral and bunkhouse?'

'Smelling out rats,' Holliday said. 'Are you going to give him up, Mr. Singer?'

'Give who up?' He looked at his son. 'Do you know what the hell he's talking about?'

'No, but I'll sure as hell get him if there's a killer on this place,' Carl said, checking the loads in his gun. 'Holliday, you and the soldier come around from behind. I'll break in the bunkhouse door and we'll surprise him, whoever it is.'

After a brief hesitation, Holliday nodded and trotted his horse over to the corral where John-Jack waited. Murray observed this from the porch and said, 'If they jump Satchel, he'll yell his head off. What he could say wouldn't be pretty.'

'He ain't going to get a chance to say it,' Carl assured him, and left the porch, trotting toward the bunkhouse. He waved his hands, first in one direction, then the other, and Holliday and the sergeant skirted the building to come in behind.

A group of hands came from the barn and watched Carl kick the door open with his foot. Then he burst inside and there was a roll of gunfire and a man's long, surprised yell.

Holliday had to batter at the rear door with his shoulder before the latch tore away, and he staggered into the room, trying to catch his balance. Carl was standing over Satchel; he rolled him over with his toe and looked at the man's face.

'He went for his gun as soon as I came in,' Carl said. 'Who'd have thought it!' He looked at Holliday. 'Where's the sergeant?'

It was a good question, and annoyed Ben, because he gave John-Jack credit for having a little guts. But instead the man had hung back. He came now to the doorway, looked in, then shrugged and leaned his shoulder against the frame.

'You have one, M'sieu Holliday. Now where is the other?'

'What other?' Carl Singer asked.

DuJoise held up two fingers. 'The other who was with him.' He pointed to Satchel. 'I am always curious, m'sieus, why a man walks when he can ride. His horse is not lame. I looked.' He left the doorway and rolled Satchel face down, then more closely examined the badly burned seat of Satchel's pants. 'A man does not sit in a fire. Did he fall? Or was he knocked down?'

'Where's Satchel's gun?' Holliday asked. 'You said that he went for it.'

'Well, he stuck his hand under the mattress,' Carl said. 'I just guessed he was after a gun. What did you expect me to do? Wait and see?' He turned as a shadow darkened the door, and Murray Singer stepped inside. 'It was Satchel, Dad.'

'Mmmm,' Murray said. 'It doesn't surprise me none.' He looked at Ben Holliday. 'What are you pawing under the mattress for?'

'His gun. Here.' He lifted it to his nose and sniffed it, then handed it to John-Jack.

109

'Recently cleaned and oiled,' the sergeant said. Then he turned impatiently. 'There is nothing more here, m'sieu.' He stepped outside.

'What's the army doing in this?' Murray asked impatiently. 'I never liked the army around my place, and I never will.'

'Take it up with Colonel Dawson,' Holliday said. 'He's my new aide.' The whole notion seemed to insult Murray Singer, and Holliday went out. Sergeant DuJoise was at the watering trough, washing his hands and face, and Holliday crossed over to him. 'Where the hell were you when I hit the door?'

'Looking in the window,' DuJoise said, grinning. 'It is surprising what a man sees through a window.' He glanced past Ben Holliday to see if anyone was near enough to hear. 'You know that Carl is lying? The dead man was on his stomach when the front door was opened. He rolled on his side and made no move at all when Carl shot him.'

'You're sure of that?'

'I will swear it. And the gun under the mattress, it was too well oiled. A man does not dismantle his pistol and oil it while leading his horse, m'sieu.'

'By God, that's so.'

'And he was not far ahead of us,' DuJoise pointed out. 'I do not think he took the time to clean his gun, because he didn't have it.'

'That's right. And a man with his tail burned

110

isn't thinking about a clean Smith & Wesson.' He pulled his face out of shape and gnawed his lip. 'I'm going to assume that Satchel didn't kill Ollie, but knew who did. We got too close to him too quickly, Sergeant. That was my mistake.'

'And mine,' DuJoise said. Don't blame yourself.' He tapped Holliday on the arm. 'Ears coming, m'sieu.'

Holliday washed up as Murray Singer and his son came over. Murray said, 'I deeply regret this, Holliday.'

'Do you?' Holliday raised his head and let the water stream off. 'And you keep calling me Holliday, like I was some damned flunky around here. I'm *Mr.* Holliday, and don't forget it.'

A crimson rush of resentful anger stained Murray's face, and he took a cigar from his pocket and lit it as though he desperately needed something to do. Finally he said, 'You're quick to take offense, Mr. Holliday.' Then he chuckled. 'Hell, let's not argue. This whole affair has made us jumpy. Why don't you come to the house and have a drink? Stay for supper; the offer's still good. The sergeant can eat in the cookshack.'

'The cookshack?' Holliday stared at Murray Singer. 'For your information, Sergeant DuJoise was a commissioned officer in three European armies. A colonel, no less. He eats at your table if I do.'

'Of course,' Singer said. 'I'll tell the cook. Carl, you get a couple of men and get Satchel in the ground before he gets ripe.' He walked off, trailing cigar smoke, and Carl turned to the barn.

Jean Jacques DuJoise smiled. *'Merci,* m'sieu. But I was only a lieutenant.'

'The secret of getting along with Texans,' Holliday said, 'is to double everything, and triple it if you can. They liked to be impressed.' Then he laughed. 'What the hell, you'd have made a good colonel anyway.' He glanced past DuJoise, and the sergeant looked around. Betty Singer had come out and was standing on the porch. 'The last time I was here, she courted me, and I suspect for a good reason. If you've got any continental manner, John-Jack—'

'Ah, m'sieu, I am French!' He pulled his fingers together, placed them against puckered lips, and pulled them away with a loud smack. 'You wish the table to be turned, eh?'

'It's worth a try,' Holliday said. 'Five will get you ten that Murray Singer wants to own my railroad, and pay nothing for it. Still I think the deal's too big for Singer to handle alone. That'll stand some looking into.' He dried his face with a handkerchief, then they walked on to the house.

Betty remained on the porch, and she smiled as Ben Holliday took her outstretched hand. 'I want you to meet Colonel Jean

Jacques DuJoise.'

'Enchanted,' DuJoise said, bringing his heels together with a wooden crash. He kissed her hand lingeringly, from a deep bow, and a burst of pleasure bloomed in Betty Singer's cheeks.

'But he's a sergeant.'

'Only until his commission is reconfirmed,' Holliday said smoothly.

'Well,' she said, smiling, 'you sure know how to kiss a hand, I must say.'

'Perhaps you would show me this exciting house,' DuJoise said. His glance touched Holliday. 'I take it you've seen it, m'sieu, so there is no need for you to come along.'

'Am I being excluded?' Holliday asked.

'Precisely,' DuJoise said. 'I will tell mademoiselle of Paris, which is a much more enchanting place than Chicago.' He offered his arm and she took it, laughing at Ben Holliday.

'Daddy wanted me to bring you into the study, but I guess you know the way.'

'If my tears of disappointment don't blind me,' Holliday said, and went into the house.

As they walked slowly to the shady side of the house, Betty said, 'Are you really a colonel?'

'But of course! I have fought many wars, but I would gladly fight another for you.'

'Oh, that's silly. Men shouldn't talk like that.'

'Why not? Don't your Texas men fight for

113

their women?'

'Well, yes, but it's different.'

He laughed. 'True. I use the sword instead of a pistol. I believe it is a proper weapon for defending a lady. A pistol is much too crude for her sensitive nature, all that noise and smelly powder.'

Betty Singer laughed. 'I don't know whether to believe you or not.'

'Test me.'

'What? Why, I wouldn't want you to just kill a man to prove—'

'Then you do believe I would?'

'No, I don't believe it,' she said. 'Well, maybe I do. I wouldn't want to test you, though.'

'Pick a man, and he is dead,' DuJoise said. 'M'sieu Holliday?'

This shocked her. 'Your friend?'

'He is not my friend,' he said. 'Fah! I only met him this morning, and it is only with beautiful women like yourself that I form lasting fondnesses on such short acquaintance.' He was a handsome man, smiling, charming, and behind him lay a trail of feminine conquests as long as his military record. He framed the picture with his hands as he talked. 'I would pick a suitable time to challenge him, being of course most discreet so that no one ever suspected you were connected in any way. Perhaps I would find a flaw in the way he held his fork; I'm easily offended by vulgar manners. A slap across the face with a glove, lightly, of course, would bring him to his feet in a most insulting manner. He would challenge me, and as the challenged, I'd pick the weapons. A meeting at dawn, a quick thrust home, and an honor is saved.'

'Why—why, you speak as though you'd already—planned it.' She pulled slightly away from him as though suddenly chilled. 'I—I don't want to hear any more about this.'

'As you wish, but since your brother just killed a man, I thought—well, you're more sensitive than I imagined.'

'What my brother does, I don't want to hear about,' Betty said. 'I don't understand Carl, or my father. My mother didn't either. Now I think we'd better go in.' At the door, she paused. 'The servant will show you to your room. He'll pour a bath for you if you wish it, and brush your uniform.'

'Thank you,' he said, bowing over her hand. She went down the length of the porch, and he observed her until she passed from his sight, then he walked down the hall. The study door was open and, as he passed, Murray Singer hailed him.

'Ah, come in. A drink?'

'Thank you, yes,' DuJoise said. He took the glass Murray handed him and continued to stand.

'We were talking about this unfortunate trouble,' Murray said. 'I think Mr. Holliday will agree with me that it was an unforeseen development and will be best forgotten.'

'Mr. Singer doesn't think we should call in the Texas Rangers to investigate.'

'It's a local problem,' Singer said. 'Let's handle it as that.' He spread his hands. 'We'll never know what got into Satchel, and it's just as well. Here, Mr. Holliday, let me fill your glass.'

'One's enough on an empty stomach,' Ben Holliday said. 'DuJoise, why don't you sit down? Frankly, I'm too busy with the railroad to go chasing around every time anyone gets shot. As Mr. Singer pointed out, the seeds of this thing probably were sown a long time ago, when Skinner worked here. Satchel's dead, and so is Skinner. We buried our man, and you buried yours. That's even enough.'

'Now you're talking like a Texan,' Singer said, smiling. 'You know, Ben, we've had our differences, but I believe we think alike. You're a man who has to be going somewhere. Well, so do I. I'm never satisfied with what I have. When a man gets that way, he ought to dig a hole and crawl in it.' He waved his hand. 'When I married my wife I had thirteen hundred acres and a sod hut. When I wanted more land, I took it, and if a man got in my way I stepped on him so hard you could hear him yell in the next county.'

'Then I take it you never met a man who stepped on you,' Holliday said.

116

'A few have tried,' Murray Singer admitted. He studied Holliday, then laughed. 'I can't help but measure you, because it's habit with me to measure a strong man. I don't think I'll ever get tired of testing my strength.'

Carl came down the hall, then, and into the room. He poured himself a whisky and flopped in a leather chair. 'Satchel's buried. One of his bunkhouse friends is carving a headboard. Beats me what the hell he'll put on it.' His head swung around and he looked at Jean DuJoise. 'Is the army working for the railroad now, or is it the other way around?'

'Trains fascinate me,' DuJoise said, smiling.

'That's a hell of an answer to a serious question,' Carl said.

'Mind your own business,' Murray said. 'Mr. Holliday, I hear that someone has made an offer to buy the line.'

'Yes, that's so.'

'You're considering it, I suppose.'

'I have considered it,' Ben said. 'I don't think I'm interested.'

'That hardly sounds sensible,' Carl said flatly.

'Drink your whisky and keep out of this,' Murray said. 'Well, Ben, if the offer wasn't so small it was ridiculous, I think it would pay to give it some serious thought.'

'Mr. Singer,' Ben said, 'if I think of a thing for five minutes, or for five years, it's been serious thinking. Now what would you do if

117

you were in my place? Sell out and go home whipped? Maybe I can't win, but nobody, and I really mean nobody, is going to be able to say it wasn't because I didn't put up a good fight. I've got finances for another month, at the rate I'm going. And I'll spend every last nickel, use up every piece of equipment, trying to take in ten dollars in revenue from that line. If it goes bust, the receivers can have it, then whoever buys it won't be getting such a good bargain.'

'I suppose you've considered what this is going to do to your career,' Murray said. 'You'll never rise above an assistant manager's job with any railroad. Stockholders don't like men who run their investment to a tatter, then toss it in their lap.'

'That's right,' Ben Holliday admitted. 'And I don't like to do it, but I'll tell you one thing here and now. It might be better for me if I got out of railroading, got out from under my father's thumb than to struggle on the way I've been going. If I make a railroad out of this financial wreck, how much good do you think it will do me? I work for no salary. Any profit for me will come as a dividend from the stock I hold. And, Mr. Singer, a lot of trains are going to have to travel up and down that track before I can declare a dividend.' He leaned back in his chair and surveyed Murray Singer in a frankly unfriendly manner. 'You want the line; I know that. You want it for a song, without a fight. Well, it may take a song, but

118

it'll be the dearest one you ever sang in your life. And as for the fight, Mr. Texas-Cattle-Baron, you're going to find out when this is finished that, up to now, you never knew what a real fight was.'

'That sounded like a declaration of war,' Singer said.

'Well, what the hell did you expect, peace?'

CHAPTER SEVEN

As soon as the cattle train was loaded at end of track, Ben Holliday telegraphed Dodge City for the departure time of the southbound mail train; he wanted it into the siding at Comanche so he could take the northbound straight through. He felt that this was important, to highball through without a stop, sort of a symbol of the railroad's intentions, its way of doing business. Besides, it would be the first cattle train originating in Texas, and to Holliday's way of thinking it brought just a little nearer the end of the overland cattle drives.

He sat at the small desk in the rattling, swaying caboose, composing a carefully worded telegram to be sent to his father when he reached Dodge. Sergeant Jean DuJoise slept in one of the bunks, his hat covering his face. Holliday wanted his message to sound optimistic without being boastful, for the running of this train was in no way going to affect the fate of Midland-Pacific; it was simply something that hadn't been done before.

The freight train did not rocket along at twenty-five miles an hour. Closer to ten would have been right, and when it passed through the yard at Comanche, Ben Holliday was catching up on his sleep.

He woke to the brakie's hand on his shoulder. 'We hooked this message as we passed through the yard, Mr. Holliday.' The brakie turned up the lamp so Holliday could read, then went toward the front of the car to get some coffee.

The message was short. *No poles or wire . . . no credit . . . Harry.*

Holliday crumbled it into a ball and swore softly. Jean DuJoise stirred and then said, 'Trouble, m'sieu?'

'The army is going to have to wait for their telegraph,' Ben said. 'And I hate like hell to think of telling Dawson that.'

DuJoise shrugged eloquently. 'It will not be the first time he's heard bad news.' Then he settled back, his hands behind his head. 'A pity, m'sieu. With a telegraph to the army post the job of watching the Indians would have been easier.'

'Father used to tell me that I couldn't have everything, but I still like to try.' He fell silent a moment. 'Still, it's a smart man who admits he can't go any farther, and if they won't extend credit, then I'll have to try something else.'

Just what that was, Holliday didn't know, and he was thinking about it when he went back to sleep.

The flavor of coffee and frying bacon woke him. Daylight streamed through the dirty windows, and Holliday got out of the bunk to stagger to the wash bucket. DuJoise was already up, sitting by a window, looking out on the prairie.

Suddenly he cried, 'Ah! Well done, m'sieu!'

'What the hell are you looking at?' Holliday asked, peering over his shoulder. He had to scan a moment before he caught sight of the horseman, riding full tilt toward the train. And behind the lone man, a herd of Comanches whooped and charged along in pursuit. 'He's trying to make the train!' Holliday said. Then he strained for a better look. 'That's Jim Bender! Slow the train.'

'No, no!' DuJoise said. 'He will make it. If you slow the train, the Indians will board her.' He left his seat and got his carbine and Holliday's rifle. 'But we can help him a little, eh?'

He jammed the muzzle through a window and began to fire at the Indians. This support spurred Bender on to a renewed effort, and the Indians seemed to drop back a little when Holliday's Winchester began to hammer. He wasn't hitting anything, but DuJoise scored, and Jim Bender altered his course, came alongside the train, and left the saddle. Holliday put down his rifle and went to the rear platform.

There was a momentary flicker of surprise in Bender's eyes when he saw Holliday, then he said, 'I found the Indians. You want to take a guess at what kind of luck I had?'

'No talks?'

'You are so right,' Bender said, and went into the caboose.

DuJoise was cleaning his carbine, and he grinned at the ex-marshal. 'A good ride, m'sieu.'

'Got a little warm there for a spell, John-Jack.' He looked at Ben and grinned. 'That was a mighty pretty sight, that train huffin' along the track,' He sniffed. 'Is that horseshoe coffee?' He took a cup from the rack and went forward to fill it. When he came back, he scraped his whiskered face with his fingernails, and looked at DuJoise. 'What are you doin' ridin' the railroad?'

'I am the new aide to M'sieu Holliday,' DuJoise said. 'The old one, Skinner, is dead.'

Jim Bender frowned heavily. 'Now that was kind of sudden, wasn't it?'

Holliday told him about it, and about the shooting at Singer's place. 'Of course, Satchel didn't kill Ollie. But he knew who did, and that was enough to get him shot.' He studied Jim Bender at length. 'You were once pretty thick with the Singers. For my money they're a nest of rattlesnakes, and if they buzz at me I'm going to do what I have to do. Where would you stand, Jim?'

'With you,' Bender said, 'If you didn't include Betty.'

'Jim, she's there with her father and brother. What can I do?'

123

Bender shook his head. 'I keep my business to myself, Ben, but when we broke up, it wasn't because she was like her old man or Carl. It was because she wasn't.'

'That I don't get.'

'It's simple. She never liked the way either of them grabbed land, or whatever else they wanted.'

'Then why didn't she leave?' Ben asked. 'You wanted to marry her, didn't you, Jim?'

'Yep. But good or bad, they're her family, Ben, and she's loyal to 'em.' He finished his coffee. 'Ben, I'd ride with you against Murray and Carl, and take my chances that Betty would forgive me for it. You've made up your mind that Murray's after the line?'

'Yes, but I think he has partners,' Holliday said. 'I don't want a fight until they're all smoked out in to open.' He sat there deep in thought for a minute. 'No chance of getting the Indians to talk, huh?'

Bender shook his head. 'They know a train went south, and as far as they're concerned, it was a breach of faith. Sorry, Ben, you'll just have to fight 'em. Better arm your train crews. They may try to stop the next one going south.'

'You really think so?' Ben asked, his voice hopeful.

Bender's curiosity was aroused. 'Ben, do you want that kind of a fight? It might drag out until winter.'

'No, but it's good to know that I can get the

Indians together whether they like it or not.'

Bender glanced at Sergeant DuJoise. 'Do you know what that means? I don't.'

The Frenchman's shoulders rose and fell. 'Who knows the thinking of a general?'

*   *   *

The last thing Ben Holliday expected when he arrived at Dodge was a celebration; the town seemed to go mad, and a brass band came marching onto the track, blocking them effectively. The crowd was immense, shouting, waving their hats, firing pistols into the air, and through it all came a delegation in buggies, the mayor and all the city officials, and a swarm of cattle buyers, all eager to sign checks and pay top prices.

Holliday, with Bender and DuJoise in tow, was whisked away by buggy and taken to a suite of rooms at the hotel. A bartender served and two waiters passed the drinks around to the jam of frock-coated men, Harry Lovell was there, but had no chance to talk to Holliday; the best Lovell could manage was a smile and a wave of the hand from across the room.

'A sterling achievement,' the mayor said, raising his glass. The bankers with him nodded, and everyone took his whisky neat. 'Perhaps, Mr. Holliday, you would consent to answer a few questions for us.'

'Why not?'

The mayor clapped his hands for silence. 'Gentlemen, Mr. Holliday has consented to answer our questions. Would you step right over there, sir, where everyone can see you. Thank you. As you are well aware, gentlemen, the success of Midland-Pacific has a direct bearing on our city. So does its failure, but today we are talking of success. Mr. Holliday, are you ready for the questions?'

'Yes,' Ben said, and accepted a cigar and a light; he hoped it would cover his nervousness and make him appear as though he had done this many times.

One of the bankers had a question. 'Mr. Holliday, you have done what two other men failed to do, bring a train from end of line to Dodge. Can we conclude from this that Midland-Pacific has resolved her difficulties?'

'No, you may not,' Ben said. 'However, we're working on them.'

Another man asked, 'Is there any truth to the rumor that you've accepted additional capital?'

'No additional capital has been offered. So we could hardly accept it.' Another man was bidding for attention. 'Yes?'

'Do you plan to run a freight on schedule?'

Holliday smiled. 'I'd like to run one twice a day, but I hardly think business warrants it. In a few days, another train will come north with Box X steers, and return, I hope, with freight. Military supplies for Fort Elliot, and freight of

126

any nature to ranchers along the line will be accepted.'

'Do you have a solution for the Indian trouble this is bound to create, sir?'

'Yes,' Ben said. 'Fight.'

There was some laughter, then Holly Bristow said, 'Mr. Holliday, I don't believe I've ever met you, but since you've exhibited such frankness with us here, perhaps you'll answer my question: did you receive a legitimate offer for the line?'

'Yes.'

Bristow smiled. 'Are you going to accept it, sir?'

'I am not,' Ben Holliday said. A murmur of surprise rippled among them, then died. Then Holliday asked, 'Did you make the offer, sir?'

A cattle buyer laughed and said, 'He's got you there, Bristow.'

Bristow colored and hesitated. 'I made the offer, yes, but as representative for a group of men.'

'Would you care to name them?' Ben asked.

'No, sir, I would not.'

'And why not? He smiled. 'If the offer is as legitimate as you say, sir, then public knowledge of their names could harm no one.'

'I'm not at liberty to do so,' Bristow said. 'You've answered my question; thank you.'

'But you haven't answered mine,' Holliday said flatly.

'No, and I'm not going to,' Bristow said,

127

sitting down.

'Perhaps I can answer it for you,' Ben said. 'Murray Singer, Bert Hutchins, and I think Jerry Vale.' Singer he was sure of, and Hutchins was a good bet, but Vale had been a guess based on the close friendship of the three in Singer's study. And Bristow's dropped jaw told Holliday that he had scored in the X ring.

'You had no right to do that.' Bristow said coolly. 'No right at all.'

'It's my railroad,' Holliday said.

'But it may not be for long,' Bristow said, and stalked out of the room.

There were a few more questions, and Holiday answered them honestly, then the gathering broke up, except for a portly, mustached man. He waited until the others had gone, then said, 'I'm Swinner, Western Union. I refused you the poles and wire, Mr. Holliday.'

Ben didn't want to argue about it. 'You acted wisely for your company, Mr. Swinner. I was going to gamble with your equipment.'

Swinner glanced at DuJoise and Jim Bender. 'I'd like to talk to you alone, if I may.'

'Consider us alone,' Holliday said. 'They're close associates.'

Swinner shrugged and sat down, crossing his legs. 'Have it your way, Mr. Holliday. I don't suppose, since I turned you down on the poles and wire, that you'd care to tell me what you

128

were going to do.'

'Why not? I was going to make a connection with Fort Elliot.'

'Hardly profitable,' Swinner said. 'We've been asked to put in a line also. Too costly, running poles parallel to your right of way. Of course, if you'd give us an easement—'

Ben Holliday shook his head. 'We use the telegraph for business and write off the expense of it. You're in business to make a profit off of what always is a loss to us. Sorry, no easement.'

'Let me point out to you,' Swinner said, 'that if you do foot the bill for a line to Elliot, all you'll get out of it is some help with the Indians. That won't last forever. Then where's your investment?'

'Well at least I got something for it,' Holliday said. 'If Western Union wants to buy our existing poles and equipment—'

Swinner waved his hand and smiled. 'No, I don't think so. However, we'd take this millstone from around your neck, and in return build the line to Fort Elliot for you. Naturally you'd use the line at the established railroad rate.'

Ben Holliday laughed softly. 'That's certainly decent of the company, Mr. Swinner, but it hardly meets the demands of Midland-Pacific.'

'Oh? What do you suggest?'

'Midland-Pacific will pursue plans for

129

expansion until the doors are locked by the receivers. Any agreement entered into would have to include areas of expansion.'

Swinner shook his head. 'We'll string wire to Fort Elliot and take the rest off your hands. That's our offer, Mr. Holliday. We're not going to buy easements until our till is pumped dry.'

'We wouldn't want Western Union to go broke,' Holliday said. 'I think Midland-Pacific could provide easements along our right of way. However, we have operators who shouldn't be put out of a job just because the operation changes hands.'

'We hire and train our own operators,' Swinner said. 'I'm sure the company wouldn't absorb your labor force.'

Holliday ignored this. 'And there would have to be a time clause in the contract, Mr. Swinner. That is to say, once the contracts are signed, construction of the Fort Elliot line would have to start immediately and be finished without interruption. This would prevent anyone from fulfilling the letter of the contract by starting, and getting off the hook by not finishing.'

'That hardly sounds trustful,' Swinner said.

'It's business. Naturally you'd be protected by an automatic easement on any right of way Midland-Pacific acquires. And I think poles ought to go up as the rails go down.'

'You're not considering our other

schedules.'

'I'm considering the fact that if Midland-Pacific loses, so do you. Now about existing lines, and so forth. I think that under these terms, twenty thousand would be a fair price. That's a third of material and labor cost.'

Swinner whisled, then said, 'Now you've made me lose interest.'

'Why don't you talk it over? I'll be in Dodge until tomorrow evening. Give me an answer then.'

'All right, but I'm afraid you've pressed it too far. Look, Holliday, I'm a reasonable man. Let me out from under on your labor force, and I'll present the offer.'

'Done,' Ben said, and shook hands.

After he stepped out, Jim Bender sighed and rubbed his stomach. 'That wasn't much different from courthouse politics. You ought to run for Congress, Ben.'

'Thanks, no.'

'What's Western going to do about the wires strung to Singer's place?' Bender asked.

'Tear them down, probably,' Holliday said.

'Ain't you got contracts with Singer and Hutchins and Vale?'

'Sure,' Ben said. 'Contracts with three men who want my railroad. What do you want me to do, Jim? Go on honoring the agreements?'

'I would,' Bender said. 'Even if it cost me.'

'And that's why you're not running a railroad,' Holliday said. 'If it just cost me, personally, then maybe I'd stick it out. But with the railroad at stake, I'd cut a man's throat from ear to ear to save it.'

'I guess,' Bender said. 'You save it and you save yourself, then you can report back to your pappy that you're a whoppin' success.'

'Oh, hell, there's more to it than that!'

'Sure there is; I never doubted it.' He turned to the door. 'I'm going to get me a bath and a shave, then about six drinks in a row.'

'Jim, you're not mad, are you?'

'Naw, but I've learned that one side of the fence is no cleaner than the other. You comin' along, John-Jack?'

'I stay with M'sieu Holliday.' He shrugged. 'I'm in the middle.'

'No man's in the middle,' Jim Bender said.

Holliday stared at him. 'That's kind of a switch for you, isn't it Jim?'

'Well, I guess when a man wants to get off the fence, the best way is just to jump.'

He went out and DuJoise said, 'A good man but bound by his own principles. To live, a man must be a little bit of the coward one day, a wise man the next, a hero another day, and a fool the day after. And all without a twinge of conscience. M'sieu is hot or cold, good or bad, never in between. It was his trouble with the woman; he wanted her to be all one way. It can't be done.'

They went down to the lobby to get a room, and found that the one they had been in had been rented for them. Holliday ordered bath water brought up, and a meal, then went out to make arrangements for a tailor to fit him for a suit of clothes.

When he got back to the room, he found Harry Lovell waiting in the hallway. 'I'm sorry,' Lovell said. 'I tried, Ben.'

'That's all a man can do. Don't moon about it. Come on in.'

He closed the door and heard DuJoise singing in the adjoining room. Then he came out, clad in the lower half of his underwear, toweling himself dry. Two vivid scars crossed his chest, old saber wounds, Holliday imagined, then tried to imagine himself facing cold steel—and couldn't. That called for a particularly acute sense of courage in a man, a kind he didn't have.

'Sit down, Harry. Sergeant, this is Mr. Lovell, my accountant. Sergeant John-Jack DuJoise.'

The two shook hands, then Lovell sat down and lit a cigar. The tailor came, and DuJoise let him in. While the man took measurements and displayed his samples, Holliday and Harry Lovell talked.

'I never saw Dodge stirred up,' Lovell said. 'To look at it, you'd think something really important happened.' He reached into his pocket for some papers. 'The cattle buyer accepted our head count and made out the draft. It's good to have a little money for a change.'

'Take a good look at it,' Holliday said. 'We won't have it tomorrow. You'd better take this down, Harry. I want an order of thirty-five ton of rail sent out before supper. And see what you can do about ties; we'll use all we have. I want to put this siding in; running one train at a time is foolish. And send a wire to my brother, Adam. Ask him if he can come out here for two weeks. I'm going to need some legal advice.'

'What for?' Lovell asked.

'Well there's some contracts coming up and—' A knock on the door interrupted him and DuJoise opened it. 'Well, for heaven's sake! Anna!'

'I'm sorry to intrude,' she said, smiling. Then she saw Harry Lovell, and he turned quickly and went over to the window and stood looking out. 'I heard you were here, and since—well, I thought I'd say hello.'

'What are you doing in Dodge?'

'My father came to see a lawyer about a patent,' she said. The tailor stood there, tape in hand, patience in his expression. 'You're busy. I'll talk later to you, in Comanche.'

'No, no!' He took her hand. Then he turned to the tailor. 'You've got enough there. Something in a dark brown. And not a heavy material.' He stepped into the hall and closed the door. 'Will you have a cup of coffee with me?'

134

'My father's in a room downstairs,' she said. 'Would it be all right—'

'Of course,' he said taking her arm.

As they walked down the stairs, Anna said, 'Papa and I are going to take the night mail train back. Maybe I shouldn't have interruped you.'

'If you hadn't and I found out about it, I wouldn't have forgiven you.'

This pleased her; he could tell that from the sudden warmth in her eyes. 'I do hope that man found his wife,' she said. When he frowned, she went on to explain. 'The man who was in your room talking to you. He was in the lawyer's office when Papa and I went there. The lawyer was trying to find his wife.'

'Which man?'

'The short one with the suit.'

'Harry Lovell? You must be mistaken, Anna.'

She stopped at the base of the stairs. 'I'm not. Papa thinks he works for you. Is that so?'

'Lovell's the accountant. Which lawyer did you go to?'

'Mr. Bristow.'

Somehow he felt that he knew that even before she said it, and it gave him a sickness in the stomach to know that Lovell was working against him.

Anna said, 'Is something wrong, Ben?'

'No, nothing now.'

She opened the door for him, and Fritz

Neubauer turned his head; he had been dozing in the chair. When he saw Ben Holliday he stood up and straightened his coat and unconsciously wiped the palm of his hand on his pant leg. 'Papa, this is Mr. Holliday.'

'So much a pleasure,' Neubauer said, shaking hands. He was ill at ease, unsure of himself or what he should say or how he should act. 'Anna spoke of you. My English is not good.'

'It's fine,' Ben said. His glance touched Anna Neubauer briefly. 'Would you excuse me, for say ten or fifteen minutes?'

'I say something wrong?' Neubauer asked.

'No, no,' Ben assured him. 'I've got to talk to Lovell now, Anna. It's the way I am; I can't leave a thing go, or wait.'

'I understand,' she said.

When he turned to the door, Neubauer said, 'You come, you go. I say something bad?'

'Explain it to him,' Ben said, and went out.

As he made the top of the stairs, he saw Lovell walking toward him; Lovell stopped and said, 'You didn't stay long.'

'Do you feel nervous, Harry?'

'No.'

'Guilty?'

'Why should I?'

'Did you ever find your wife, Harry?'

Lovell laughed. 'Hell, you know I'm not married. So she said she saw me. What of it?'

'Tell me what you and Bristow had to talk

136

about, Harry.'

'A private matter, Ben. Believe me.'

'Sorry, but I just can't do that now. Bristow represents interests that want me to go broke. You come to Dodge to see Swinner and you talk to Bristow first. What did you say to Swinner, Harry? Did you tell them I was broke, that I was going to stay broke? Or did you show them my balance sheets with red ink at the bottom?'

'You're accusing me without proof,' Lovell said. 'On the word of a foreigner.' He shook his head and laughed. 'I've worked for your father nearly eighteen years. You don't scare me, Ben, because I'll be working for him when you're through.'

'Harry, you're through now.'

'*You're* firing me?'

'As of now.' He looked steadily at Lovell, as though sorry about this. 'Would you tell me why, Harry?'

For a moment it seemed that Lovell was going to go on denying this, but then he shrugged and said, 'For money. What the hell else?' He reached out and tapped Ben on the chest. 'They've got you, son. Make it easy on yourself. That's why I went along with Bristow; I'm too old a man to lose.'

'You were going to keep your job, is that it?'

'Yes, and a nice bonus.' He sighed. 'Why don't you just hit me, Ben? I'd feel better.'

'Would it do any good? The damage is

done. Singer knows all my business now.'

'Your father too. I've been writing him letters. Not bad letters. He only wants to know how you're getting along.'

'This is my railroad to run. It's about time he got his damned hand off the throttle. Go on back to Chicago, Harry. He'll give you a job and a gold watch for all those eighteen years of faithful service.'

Lovell shook his head. 'Eighteen years are a lot of years. Too long to work for one man.' He sighed and found a cigar in his pocket and lit it. 'You know, I've been dreading the day when you found out; I like to think of myself as an honorable man. That must sound like a lie to you, after my selling you out. But I did it for the railroad.'

'Get the hell away from me,' Ben said flatly. 'Get far away, Harry. And I'll tell you something else: don't say good-bye to Holly Bristow. I'll do that for you, right now.'

'He only looks soft,' Lovell warned.

'That'll make it all the more interesting,' Holliday said, and went down the stairs, two at a time. As soon as he reached the street, he asked a man where Bristow's office was, then cut toward it, his stride long and determined.

138

CHAPTER EIGHT

Holly Bristow was studying some legal papers when Ben Holliday opened the office door with a crash and stood there. Bristow looked up, then motioned for him to come in. 'You're going to bring me trouble, I suppose?'

'I just fired Harry Lovell,' Ben said.

Bristow shrugged. 'That was a fool thing to do.'

'I don't want any spies in my outfit!' Holliday snapped.

Bristow threw down his pencil and leaned back in his chair. 'Mr. Holliday, you don't have the situation in hand at all. You're on the ragged edge of being on the run, if you aren't there already. Now if you'd used your head, you'd have kept your mouth shut and never let on to Lovell that you knew about his arrangement. That way you'd have kept tabs on him, and used him more than he used you. What are you going to do for an accountant, Holliday? Who knows as much about your finances and business as Lovell?' He spread his hands and smiled. 'Now you threw it all away because you stopped thinking. You know something, I think you're going to be easier to beat than Singer thinks, because you can be made to go off half cocked.'

The fact that he was right angered Holliday,

and even as he felt it rise in him, he knew that he was going to do something even more foolish than fire Harry Lovell. He stepped up to Bristow's desk and said, 'I feel like knocking your head off.'

'Aw, now you couldn't be that stupid,' Bristow said. He looked at Holliday for a moment, then sighed and got up. As he came around his desk, he said, 'I suppose you boxed in college?'

'I did.'

Bristow started to take off his coat. 'We don't use those rules out here.' Then he whipped the coat back on and hit him, taking Holliday completely by surprise. He spun half around and fell across Bristow's desk, then shook his head and straightened up.

He started to raise his hands, to assume a posture of defense, but Bristow bent down, came in under Holliday's uplifted hands, and caught him with a belting hook in the stomach. Ben brought his fist down and struck Bristow on the back of the neck, not hard enough to hurt him, but enough to break the rhythm of Bristow's attack.

Holliday was forced to give ground, to back up when he wanted to carry the fight to Bristow, and it was going to be Bristow's fight; he could tell that much, and it was a sickness in his mind, to know that he was going to get licked.

He had the courage to stand up to Bristow

140

and take it, and he went down three times, but he always managed to come back. And he even managed to hurt Bristow a little, opening a cut on his eyebrow and lip, but it wasn't enough. Bristow could hit, and he followed no set of rules, no pattern of fighting; he just came in close and chopped with his fists, and the blows were full of power, against which Holliday's stylized defense was useless.

After being flung back against the wall and feeling his legs wilt, Ben Holliday found that he couldn't get up. He wanted to and tried to, but the strength wasn't there. Holly Bristow turned to a side table and soaked a towel in the water pitcher. He wiped his face, then threw it at Holliday.

'Do you want to try again, Mr. Holliday?' Then he laughed. 'Clean yourself up; you look like hell!' He turned to his desk and sat down, his head pillowed in his hands.

Holliday put the towel to his face and felt better, then he looked at Bristow and wondered if the man had a headache; he hoped so. Ben Holliday wanted him to have something, anyway.

'I don't understand you,' Bristow said, daubing at his cut lip. 'You fight for this piddling railroad like it was all you had. So what the hell if you lose it? You'll go back to Chicago and your old man will give you a good job anyway. From the beginning I couldn't see why you wanted to hang on. Haven't you got

141

sense enough to know that money's going to beat you? The stock's worthless, or practically worthless, and you don't have enough cash to buy a wagonload of ties.'

Ben Holliday got up and leaned against the wall; he threw the towel in the corner and straightened his clothing. 'Bristow, if the line's so worthless, why do Singer and the others want it?'

The attorney shrugged. 'I don't know and don't care. As long as I get my commission, it stays that way. Holliday, I'm not against you personally. I just represent a client.'

'Maybe I ought to get a lawyer,' Holliday said, and went out.

His stomach muscles ached from the sting of Bristow's fists, and he took care not to take any sudden or deep breaths until the soreness left him. Harry Lovell was standing on the hotel porch when Holliday crossed over.

Lovell said, 'I wanted to tell you, Ben, that you couldn't lick him, but I don't think you'd have listened.'

'No, I wouldn't have,' Holliday said. 'Harry, you're out of it now. What's my chances?'

'Of besting the Singer bunch?' Lovell shook his head. 'On guts, you're ahead, Ben, but this time the money's going to count. And Singer's got you there. He's going to buy you out, so why not take it now and be done with it? I realized this some time ago.' He took Holliday by the arm. 'Ben, I know why you've got to do a good job but believe me, your father isn't going to hold it against you if you fail. He's right: you've got to take one good licking in your life, and the earlier the better.'

'It must be good,' Holliday said, 'to be able to see so clearly. I'm sorry, but I can't.'

His intention had been to go to his room, but he changed his mind and walked down the street to the Western Union office. He still had his brother's check, which he cashed, then added two hundred dollars of his own money; the whole thing was deposited, then he composed a message.

Adam Holliday
Fischer Bldg.
Chicago, Illinois
Buy five hundred M-P stock in my name . . .
urge you to beg, borrow, or steal to buy all
you can . . . Lovell discharged this date . . .
Need you here on important legal matters . . .
Can you come?

Ben

As he walked back to the hotel, he considered this move. Midland-Pacific had not moved on the market for six months, and he was certain that any buying would cause a flurry of interest. He knew how closely investors watched the market, even the stocks that seemed dead, and this brief bit of buying would sharpen their attention. After all, they

143

didn't know what was going on, and if Adam could come through with some money of his own, it might inspire others to invest. Then the stock would take a jump in price and some bull would hop in and hope to buy cheap and sell high. But Holliday didn't care about that. He just wanted to force the price up to where Singer's present offer would be laughable.

Maybe he will end up owning it, Holliday thought as he walked back to the Hotel. But he'll sure as hell pay more than thirty-five cents a share.

He felt good enough to smile about it, and when he stepped inside his room, Jim Bender looked up from the casino game he had going with Sergeant DuJoise.

'For a man who's been in a fight, you seem happy about it,' Bender said dryly.

'I got licked,' Holliday said. He wet a cloth and held it to the bruises on his face. 'I was smiling about something else. Jim, are you much of a horse trader?'

'Tolerably good. Why?'

'Suppose you had a horse that was a little wind broke, and you wanted to get top price, or a little better. How would you go about it?'

'There's nothin' like biddin' to raise a price,' Bender said. 'Especially when a man thinks he's getting something for nothing.'

'The stock market works the same way,' Holliday said. 'If I can get up a little buying of Midland-Pacific stock, I think I can raise the market price.'

'What good's that goin' to do you?'

'The higher the stock goes, the more expensive it's going to be for Singer to buy me out.' He pulled a chair around and sat down. 'Look, I got a cattle train into Dodge, didn't I? The newspapers will pick that up, and my father will blow it around, and when the market opens tomorrow and a thousand shares are picked up, it'll make the investors wonder if something isn't about to break out here.'

'Yeah, your back,' Bender said. 'For Christ's sake, can't you see that Singer and the others only shipped with you because they want the top price for their beef? Hell, once their range is clean, they'll throw that contract in your face and leave you sitting there, extended to the limit. Hell, you need them, Ben. If they don't ship on your line, you go broke.'

'That's the core of the whole mess, isn't it? Well, Jim, I'm going to make them see that the shoe's on the other foot. They need me!'

'Cattle have always been driven to market,' Bender said. 'Sure it's expensive and it takes time, but that's an out you can't close off.' He sighed and gave up the card game.

'Who do you know that will take a gamble?' Ben asked.

'How much of a gamble?'

'Long odds against winning, but if we get lucky, you'd make a small fortune.' He painted a clear picture for Jim Bender. 'I just wired my brother to buy five hundred dollars' worth of Midland stock. It'll open an eye or two, but not enough. I need a thousand more, or two thousand. With that much I could push the market value up.'

'A man could lose his shirt puttin' his money in your railroad.'

'Yes, and he could win the coat and pants and all the rest,' Ben said. Then he slapped his side and turned away. 'Do I sound like I'm grabbing at straws, Jim? Well I am. I've got a good roadbed and good rolling stock, if I could only get the blasted wheels to turn.'

'Evidently Singer thinks *he* can,' DuJoise said.

Holliday glanced at him, then laughed. 'For what he wants to pay for the line, he could pull up the rails and ties, sell them along with the equipment, and make three hundred per cent profit. Then he could sell the right of way and alternate sections for more profit.'

'All you need is money,' Bender said. 'Just money.'

Someone knocked, and Holliday opened the door. A corporal stood there, then came to attention. 'Which of you is Mr. Holliday?'

'I am.'

'The colonel sends his compliments, sir, and asks you to call at Fort Dodge at your convenience.'

'All right, corporal. Within the hour.' He closed the door and fingered his puffed lip.

'Am I in trouble with the army now? All I get is trouble. Not one damned piece of good news yet.'

'Your luck is bound to change,' Bender said wryly. 'No man can always have it this bad—I don't think.'

'You're real cheering,' Holliday said, turning to the door. 'I want to be out of this town by sundown. Tell the engineer, and go downstairs and tell Anna Neubauer and her father they can go back in the caboose.'

Bender grinned. 'It'll mean a refund on their ticket.'

'Go to blazes,' Holliday said 'Besides, Neubauer has a pass.'

He went down and through the lobby and hired a rig at the livery for his drive to Fort Dodge. The sentry stopped him and Holliday gave his name, then was passed on to the sergeant of the guard, who detailed a trooper to escort him to headquarters.

Colonel Ridgeway, like Dawson of Fort Elliot, was a string bean, with a lot of worry lines on his forehead, and prematurely gray hair. He saw that Holliday had a comfortable chair, and a good cigar, then said, 'The first train north was quite an event. I've been waiting a long time to see it. Never thought I would, though.'

'A train is just a train, Colonel, and they go where the tracks point. However, I've had a lot of trouble about that. Especially with Indians

147

and Texans.'

'There's going to be some dancing and painting over this one,' Ridgeway said. 'What does the railroad intend to do about it?'

'Dump it in Colonel Dawson's lap,' Holliday said. 'Every man to his job, sir. Ours is railroading.'

'A dispatch by courier from Dawson informed me that your attitude was very frank on the subject. All right, Mr. Holliday. I can't really quibble the point. But if the army is going to fight Indians for you, we're also going to use your railroad. I have a hundred and thirty cavalry mounts I want taken to Fort Elliot. When can they be loaded?'

'They'd better be loaded by sundown,' Holliday said. 'The train leaves then, dragging a string of empties.'

'Not all empties,' Ridgeway said. 'How large a detail do you want to accompany the horses? Fifty men?'

'One,' Ben said. 'He can ride to Elliot when we get to the closest point. The railroad will hold the horses in the cars until a detail from Fort Elliot arrives.'

'I'll have the quartermaster officer prepare the freight waybills and bring them to the train,' Ridgeway said. 'Mr. Holliday, would you mind telling me how long you think you can hang on? I've heard rumors that you were broke, that you were selling, that you were coming along nicely. It's a little confusing.'

'There is nothing wrong with Midland-Pacific that a hundred thousand dollars wouldn't cure,' Holliday said. 'But my chances of finding it are about as good as an old maid finding a man under her bed.'

'I appreciate the honest answer,' Ridgeway said.

They shook hands in parting, and Holliday drove back to town. At the hotel he found Swinner waiting.

'Fifteen thousand, Mr. Holliday. That's the best I can do'.

'When I said twenty thousand, I was doing you a favor,' Ben said.

'I can't go over fifteen,' Swinner said. 'Man, it was hard pressing to get that.'

'And I'm hard pressed to take twenty.'

'The deal's going to be lost if you don't come down.'

'I guess. But I can't take less. I've got the money spent, so to speak. What does Western Union want? A bleeding vein?'

Swinner sighed and shook his head, then brought a check out of his inner pocket. It was made out for twenty thousand, and he smiled. 'Had to make that one last try, Mr. Holliday. Company man, you know.'

'I wish I had a few,' Holliday said, and pocketed the check. He wanted to look at it, just to read the zeros, but he didn't, and settled for the pleasure of thinking about how advantageously he could spend this. It meant a siding, a badly needed siding, and he modified his original plan to buy the rails. To hell with that now. Since Murray Singer was going to renege on his contract, Holliday would beat him to it and shorten end of track by a mile. Singer would howl and seek an injunction, but there wasn't anything he could do about it, and he'd find that out.

It was too bad, he thought, that this twenty thousand was railroad money; with just five of it he could skyrocket the price of Midland-Pacific stock, push it so high that Murray Singer would just have to forget about stealing the line. The temptation to juggle the books was strong, but he put it down; he had no desire to go to the penitentiary for embezzlement.

Instead of going to his room, he knocked on Anna Neubauer's door; her father opened it and motioned Holliday inside. Anna was stretched out on the bed, resting; she swung her feet to the floor and raised her hands to her hair, to see if it was all right.

'Mr. Bender came around,' she said. 'Thank you for inviting us. We didn't want to stay over another night.'

'I'd like to take you to supper,' Ben said. 'I could have it brought to the room, if you like.'

'That would be nice,' Anna said. 'Sit down, Ben. Papa, bring that chair over here.' She studied the marks on his face. 'Have you been fighting?'

'Men do,' he said, then laughed. 'It was a foolish thing to do, but that seems to be what I do best.' He studied her a moment. 'Anna, I think you're a smart girl, so let me ask you something. Should I hang on to the railroad?'

She shook her head. 'I can't answer that.'

'Answer anyway. I want an honest opinion.'

She thought a moment, then said, 'It's first important to know why you want to go on fighting. Is it for the railroad, or for yourself?'

'I want the railroad to succeed.'

'Yes, I know. But is it the big reason? The all-important reason?'

He shook his head. 'I've got to go back to my father with the smell of success on me,' Ben said. 'He admires it in a man, the ability to do. It's the way I was raised, Anna, not to fail, and because my father expects me to fail now, I feel, more determined not to. Anna, if I have to, I'll take the whole blasted world down with me.'

'That's wrong,' she said.

'Wrong? I know it. But what can I do about it?'

Anna remained silent for a moment. 'Ben, you have to do what you know you can live with afterward. I don't think you're the kind of a man who destroys anyone else to save yourself. If it came to that, I think you'd sell the railroad.'

'I wish I felt that sure,' Holliday said softly. 'It's not easy to live when you're not sure what

151

you are, or how far you can go.' He turned to the door. 'I'll order supper.' He stepped out and collided solidly with Jim Bender. Bender said, 'I've been looking all over for you, Ben. Your operator here got word from end of track that Indians have been gatherin' all afternoon. They're camped out on the prairie and it don't look good.'

'They're not under attack?'

'No, not yet, but I wouldn't bet they won't be.' He took Holliday by the arm. 'We'd better not wait until sundown to pull out with that string of empties. You want me to tell the engineer?'

'Wait.' Holliday gave it some thought. 'The army is shipping some horses to Elliot. They won't be loaded yet.'

'God damn the horses!' Bender said, then he saw Anna standing in the room, listening. 'Pardon me. Ben, I don't think we should waste any time. Now that's the best advice I can give you.'

'Is an hour going to make that much difference, Jim?'

'It could,' he said. 'Ben, do you want to take the chance?'

'If we pull out now,' Holliday said, 'we won't have much of a supporting force. But if I can wait, take the chance, we might be able to get some army help. Jim, get a horse and ride to Fort Dodge. Explain it to the colonel and ask for thirty men. Give him an hour. I'll go and telegraph ahead that re-enforcements are on the way.'

'There's seven men out there, Ben. You're gambling with their lives.'

'Hell, don't you think I know it?' He gave Bender a shove. 'Get going. You don't have any time to waste.' He watched Bender dash to the lobby, then he turned to Anna and her father. 'I have to ask you to excuse me on the dinner.'

She came up to him and took his arms in her strong hands. 'Ben, go now. Right now.'

'I can't.'

'Can't or won't?'

'Either way, I guess it's the same.'

'Is a report to your father more important than those seven men?' She studied him critically. 'Ben, if they're dead when you get there, you'll think of it the rest of your life. I know you must gamble, but not this way. It's not right and you know it.'

'Sorry,' he said. 'I'll see you at the train.' Then he turned and ran out, pushing his way past people in the lobby.

Sergeant DuJoise was at the train, talking to the engineer, who already had steam up and an itch to push the throttle wide open. They turned when Holliday came up, and the engineer said, 'Mr. Holliday, empty I can push her to fifty miles an hour.'

'You'd blow her up,' Holliday said. 'Nobody ever goes that fast.'

153

'I'd rather blow her up tryin' than set here and valve off steam,' he said. On the other side of the tracks the army detail were holding the horses; loading wouldn't take long, but in view of this development the quartermaster officer had held up, pending word from a higher authority.

Holliday vaulted to the cab and jumped down on the other side. He saw the officer sitting on the corral fence, and waved to get his attention. 'All right, get 'em loaded! We'll pull out as soon as you're through!'

The army was organized, and shouting sergeants got their details into motion and the loading proceeded rapidly. Holliday went back to the other side of the train.

Sergeant DuJoise said, 'A problem for a man to wrestle, eh, m'sieu? Perhaps this will be the day of a new miracle, another Adobe Walls, where a handful of men hold off the Comanche nation.'

'Aw, why don't you shut up,' Holliday said. He walked up and down, feeling the cinders crunch under his boots. Damn it, what a spot for a man to be in. Just when he thought he was getting steam up, something had to puncture the boiler and let it out. Seven men against a trainload of paying freight and a chance to crawl out of the puddle of red ink. Not clear out, but up a little ways anyway.

And this whole thing could blow over without a shot being fired too; a man was a

154

fool to be panicked by a threat. And that's what it was. Just a threat. Nobody was under attack.

He remembered the look on Anna Neubauer's face and wondered how she knew so much, how she'd learned what was right and wrong so that she did more of one than the other. And Bender was no angel himself; he didn't have any right to be righteous. Only one man ran a railroad, gave the orders, accepted the responsibility, and took the credit or blame.

DuJoise and the engineer were still standing there when Holliday turned around. 'Hook the engine and tender to the caboose, and get the crew aboard, every railroad man in the yard who can shoot. Let's see if this damned thing will go fifty miles an hour.'

He just stepped back out of the way so they could get the job done. He went over to the dispatcher's shack and found the Dodge telegrapher there.

'This just came in, Mr. Holliday. End of track under attack, but they're holding off.'

'We're pulling out of a few minutes. Tomorrow, hook the cattle cars onto the passenger train. We'll pick it up in the Comanche yard.'

'That's going to make a nice smell for the passengers,' the dispatcher said.

'Do we have that many, that we have to worry about it? He turned to leave just as

Swinner came in. He had a handful of contracts and a look of impatience on his face. Holliday said, 'My signature on those is going to have to wait a week or so.'

'We gave you our check,' Swinner said. 'As chairman of the board you can make policy without consulting your father or brothers. Western Union isn't going to cheat you.'

'And I'm not going to go to South America with your check,' Ben said. A train whistle hooted wildly and he pushed past Swinner. 'I'll see you in a week when you come down on the work train.'

'According to contract, we don't have to start building the telegraph until you sign.'

Holliday took the check out of his pocket and thrust it at Swinner. 'Do you want this back? The line goes up in two weeks, or you can forget it. I can't wait for an answer, so give it to me now.'

Swinner's expression darkened a bit, then he said, 'All right, Mr. Holliday. A work train in a week.' He shook his head and grinned. 'I could be fired for this. We don't do business on faith and a handshake any more.'

'I don't have the time for a conference table,' Holliday said.

The train whistle continued to blow; it was time to leave and he dashed out and ran across the switchyard. The brakie had his lantern in hand although it was not yet dark, and the engineer and fireman were in the cab.

DuJoise yelled, 'Bender is not here!'

'We'll go without him,' Ben said. 'Likely he'll knock my head off for running off and leaving him. All right let's get out of here!' He swung into the engineer's cab as the throttle was cracked, and the driving wheels spun briefly before grip was made. They pulled clear of the yard and were heading for the last switch when Holliday looked around and saw Jim Bender flogging his horse, trying to catch up with the train. He watched as Bender came alongside the tender, made the jump, then came down into the cab.

'How the hell did you get to the post and back so quick?' Ben asked.

Jim Bender grinned. 'I didn't go all the way there. I got to thinking and decided that you wouldn't wait. You just ain't the kind who'd do a thing like that, Ben. So I turned around and come back.'

'We've got thirteen men aboard,' Holliday said. 'That's one hell of a force to repulse an Indian attack.'

'Well, they can't shoot through the sides of the caboose and push the engine off the track,' Bender said. He took out his tobacco and rolled a smoke, bracing himself against the side of the cab.

The engineer passed through the last switch and eased the throttle open. The pound of the drivers increased in tempo and the train rocked along, swaying and jolting on the

157

roadbed. 'How fast will this thing go?'

'The engineer says fifty miles an hour.'

Bender whistled. 'That's too damned fast for any man to go.' He studied the throttle and the engineer's hand there. 'But if he took out that screw there, the one that's keeping the throttle from goin' too far, we might hit fifty-five.'

CHAPTER NINE

As soon as the telegrapher left Murray Singer's house, the boss of Lazy T leaned back in his chair and smiled thinly. Carl Singer started to get up, and his father said, 'Sit down, sit down. You've got no place to go.' He bit off the end of a cigar and lit it. 'There must be a hell of a lot of excitement at end of track, with seventy Comanches storming those tents. I've got twenty dollars that says they don't last two hours.'

'I could take twenty men and get there in time,' Carl said.

His father looked at him. 'What would you want to do that for? The railroad is supposed to come to our rescue, not the other way around. Besides, Holliday's got considerable equipment there, and he can't afford to lose any of it.'

'You'll have to square this with Holliday afterward,' Carl said.

'Hell, do you think I worry about that? If he comes around here looking for trouble, we'll push him right off the face of Texas.' He turned his head as Betty stopped in the doorway. 'Carl and I are talking.'

'I heard some of it,' Betty Singer said. 'Dad, are the Indians attacking the camp at end of track?'

'That's what the telegrapher says.'

'Then why aren't you riding to help them?'

'It's railroad business.'

'Ten years ago when the Comanches were raiding, it was everyone's business.'

'Times have changed,' Murray Singer said. 'Betty, I wish you wouldn't bother with it now. I'm the one who has to decide.'

'Because you want a railroad? Because there isn't any more land for you to take, you want a railroad? Dad, I put my own desires aside once to take your side, yours and Carl's. Don't make me sorry for that now.'

'You're talking like a fool woman,' Murray said. 'When you gave Bender up, that was your doing, not mine. Your choice, not mine. Don't make me the goat for it now.'

'I see,' Betty said. 'You're not to blame, is that it?' She turned to the hall and stopped. 'I've wasted my loyalty, haven't I?'

She didn't wait for an answer, just went down the and out the side door. The last light of day was casting long grayish shadows in the yard as she crossed to the barn.

The Mexican hostler came forward, hat in hand.

Betty said, 'Saddle my horse, Luz.'

Then she stood there while the light faded. From across the flats three horsemen came on at a dead run, and they swung off by the barn. Jerry Vale said, 'I saw more Indians this morning than I care to think about. Your father in the house?'

'Yes.'

Bert Hutchins said, 'They've stopped work on the telegraph line, so I supposed they were hittin' the railroad.' He looked around and saw no particular activity in the yard. 'Ain't your dad goin' out?'

'I think he wants to finish his cigar first,' Betty said.

Both Vale and Hutchins looked strangely at her, then the hostler brought up her horse and she was boosted into the sidesaddle. Vale said, 'This is a poor time to go riding.' Then he shrugged and stepped back. 'None of my business. You Singers always did do what you wanted to do.'

She left the yard at a run, then Bert Hutchins said, 'Let's go to the house.' He glanced at his foreman. 'Stick around here, Rex. We likely won't be long.'

As they approached the house, Carl Singer came to the door. 'I thought I heard horses ride in. The old man's in the study. You hear about the Indians?'

'We guessed,' Vale said. 'That's why we came over, to do what we can.'

'The place was quiet when we rode in,' Hutchins said, 'we thought you'd already gone.' He stepped into the study, and Murray Singer waved his hand toward the liquor cabinet; they helped themselves.

'I heard that,' Murray said. 'Where's your

161

brains? Let the Indians have the railroad. We only want the rails and equipment anyway.'

'That's kind of hard to take,' Vale admitted. 'I've fought Indians, and I hate like hell to think we just stood by and—'

'If you're going to whine, go home,' Murray said flatly. 'Son, pour me a whisky. Well, we know what Holliday is going to do about the Indians. Fight 'em. He'll get licked. That crew of his is fine for setting railroad spikes, but no good fightin' Indians.' He turned to his son, saying, 'Go tell Betty to make us some coffee.'

Bert Hutchins said, 'She rode out just as we walked to the house.'

Murray Singer's frown warned them that he wasn't in the mood for jokes. 'What the hell do you mean, she rode out? Go take a look, Carl.'

'It's a fact,' Jerry Vale said. 'She was heading toward end of track. What's the matter with you, Murray? You sick or something?'

'That stupid female!' Singer said. 'Carl, catch up a horse and go after her before she gets killed.'

'Hell, I couldn't catch her now.'

Murray picked up a book and threw it at him, and Carl twisted so that it bounced off his shoulder. He got up and said, 'It looks like Lazy T is going to fight Indians after all. I'll get the men together.' Carl looked at his father. 'I want to see you there too.' He walked over to a cupboard and took out a holstered pistol with a cartridge belt wound around it. He tossed this in his father's lap. 'Somehow it just bothers me, all of us getting killed off and leaving you sitting there, so smart and rich. I've taken your orders and guff for a long time. Now let's go.'

For a moment Murray hesitated, then he pushed himself erect. As he put on the gun belt, he said, 'If you don't watch yourself, Carl, you're going to show a shard of decency.'

'Listen to who's talking.' Carl Singer laughed. 'I know what I am and it's all right with me.' He glanced at Vale and Hutchins. 'We're all alike; we'd steal the pennies off a dead man's eyes. So we're land hogs, money hogs, power hogs. Do we have to act like sons of bitches within our own families?'

He dashed out of the house and ran toward the bunkhouse, calling loudly to the men in the bunkhouse and barn.

Jerry Vale looked at Murray Singer, then said, 'I never thought about this before, but you make me nervous as hell. One of these days I expect you to turn on me. I guess I'd have to kill you if you did that.' Then he touched Bert Hutchins on the arm and they went out to wait by their horses.

*   *   *

Ben Holliday worked up a fine sweat, stoking the engine, keeping the fire roaring, keeping the pressure up as the train rocketed along the roadbed. Jim Bender spelled him at times; and they worked like mechanical men, backs bent, arms swinging as they sailed fuel into the open maw of the firebox. When the engineer began to lean on the whistle cord, both men raised up, and then the brakes were applied hard and the train lurched to a wheelsliding halt.

The work train from the wire-stringing crew blocked the last stretch of end of track, and they jumped down and ran alongside the cars. Bender sided Holliday and DuJoise brought up the rear, while the train crew followed a distance back.

Bender pointed to the flat prairie, but the gesture was wasted; Ben Holliday had already seen the Indians camped there. Kisdeen came to meet them.

'By God, I'm glad to see you,' he said. 'How many men you got?'

'Better than a dozen,' Holliday said. He looked around the camp and saw that Kisdeen had already done a creditable job of fortifying the place. Railroad ties were banked around the telegrapher's tent and the cook tent, and the water supply was well guarded. Holliday asked, 'Have they started shooting yet?'

'Well, not for keeps,' Kisdeen said. 'Some of the younger bucks have come in whoopin' and yellin' and showing off how brave they are. They've taken a few pot shots, but we're saving our ammunition.'

'That's smart,' Bender said. He squinted at the sky and judged the remaining daylight. 'Might not be anything doing tonight. In the morning, you'll see twice as many out there. The word's out, and they'll gather like flies around an outhouse.'

'*Oui,*' DuJoise said. 'And then, m'sieus, you will find your defenses inadequate.' He pointed to the barricades. 'With this type of a defense, the Indians can surround you easily, which is the way they like to fight. I would suggest you move your water and supplies to the trains. Tonight, of course, when it is dark and movement will be unobserved. Spread your men out along the length of the train and make them attack in a line. If they do that, you have the advantage. And if they choose to ride along the length of the train, the odds are with you even more.'

'Suppose they hit the train in a wedge and break through?' Kisdeen asked.

'They can't jump across the train,' Holliday said. 'A line of men, yes, but not the train. I think DuJoise has the best plan. Good military procedure.'

'We will wait until dark to move supplies and water,' DuJoise said.

'They won't attack tonight,' Bender said. 'We can post guards and get some sleep. But at dawn we'll have our work cut out for us.'

Bender and DuJoise began to supervise the activity around the camp, while Ben Holliday and Kisdeen talked. 'I hate to think of morning,' Kisdeen said. 'We've got to make peace with the Indians, not fight 'em. How much chance do you think we'll have after tomorrow?'

'We may not be around to worry about it,' Holliday said, and drew a frown from the maintenance super. 'Emil, do you want to please everyone? Let's work for the railroad and step on the toes of anyone who gets in the way. I made a deal with Western Union; they're taking over our existing telegraph lines and stringing new wire to Fort Elliot. Seeing that we don't have the funds to develop the lines, I thought it best to make the deal.'

'That'll throw a lot of our men out of work.'

'They can get other jobs, or stay on with Midland in other capacities. What the hell, am I supposed to hold up progress for someone's job?' He shook his head. 'I left a string of cars on the siding at Dodge; there's a shipment of army horses for Fort Elliot. So tell the brakie, engineer, and fireman to get out of here with the engine and caboose we came down on.'

'Send them back to Dodge?'

'Why not?' He tapped Kisdeen on the chest. 'We'll fight the Indians. And by the time they get back, we'll have licked them or they'll have licked us. Either way, it doesn't make much difference to the railroad; cars will still be rolling.'

'You're the boss,' Kisdeen said. Then he

grinned. 'And you're turning into a pretty good one. You won't last, but likely you'll kick up one hell of a dust cloud while you're around.'

He walked back along the line of cars, and Ben Holliday went over to the cook tent where supper was in the making. DuJoise was eating a cold potato, and he spoke when Holliday came up. 'Can I offer some advice, m'sieu le boss?'

'Advise away.'

'There are more pick handles in this camp than bullets. I've looked around, and I'd say there was no more than twenty rounds per man.'

'That's not surprising news,' Holliday said 'They'll just have to shoot straighter and less often. What's the advice, John-Jack?'

'Pick out the best shots and put them near the engine. The Indians will attack there first; they think it is alive, or a thing of evil. Do you agree?'

'All right,' Holliday said. 'Pick whoever you want.'

'You, and Bender, and myself. Perhaps three others. I'll find them before morning.' Then he laughed softly. 'It will be a noisy dawn, m'sieu'

'Who wants to die quietly?' Holliday asked.

When darkness came, they quietly transferred the water and food to the train, but took care to keep up an appearance of activity around the cookshack and telegrapher's tent.

167

Holliday sent the telegrapher away, for he could see no sense in keeping him there; any message sent would only be wasted effort, for help couldn't arrive in time to do them any good.

He joined Bender at the engine and they waited there. DuJoise finally came around with three men, sometime meat hunters who claimed they could hit what they aimed at. Bender's cigarette glowed and died as he puffed on it, his attention turned to the Indian camp out on the prairie.

They could hear the dancing and singing and see the fires dotting the flats. Bender said, 'That's poor music for a man who likes to sleep.

'This is some country,' Holliday said. 'Back in Illinois, you build a railroad, then sit back and make money. Out here you build it, then fight like hell to keep the rolling stock on the move.'

'You'd get fat in Chicago,' Bender said dryly. 'Admit it, Ben, win or lose, you've had a time of it. A lot of men go through life with nothing happening to 'em.'

'This I could skip,' Holliday said. 'To tell you the truth, I've met a German girl I'd like to know a lot better. It irritates me to have to end something before it got started.'

'You can always fire up the engine and get the hell out of here,' Bender said.

Holliday shook his head. 'The Indians

would turn on the ranchers then. No, we'll hold our ground. Run now, and it will be hell for the next man.'

'Shhhhh!' Bender said, holding up his hands. 'DuJoise, you hear anything?'

'I heard something I don't believe.'

Then the sound came to Ben Holliday, a curb chain rattling. Some man on guard duty fired his gun, and someone else shouted at him to 'put that goddamned thing away!'

They left the engine and ran over to the end of track camp as Colonel Dawson and fourteen-man detail dismounted. Lieutenant Gary was there, handling the second section, and he waved at Holliday, then attended to his duties. Dawson was peeling off his gloves and saying, 'We rode right to hell through 'em, and they let us. That bothers me.' He offered Holliday his hand, then turned as Gary came up with Betty Singer. 'We found her on the prairie.'

'When it got dark, I lost my sense of direction,' she said. Jim Bender stepped out of the shadows and she straightened a slight bit. 'Hello, Jim.'

'Come on,' Bender said softly, taking her arm. 'I'll get you some coffee.' His glance touched Dawson briefly. 'The reason you rode on through is because they wanted you here in the morning. I guess they must expect some friends tonight.'

'That's a grizzly thought,' Dawson said.

'From the fires, I'd say there were a hundred now.' He looked around to find Ben Holliday, but he was already moving off to catch up with Bender and Betty Singer.

'I don't want to intrude on you two,' Holliday said, taking Betty's free arm. 'But what are you doing out on the prairie with an Indian scare in full swing?'

'Coming here,' she said softly. 'I've changed my mind, Jim.' She looked around at him when she spoke. 'Is it too late?'

'Never too late,' he said. 'We'll talk about it over coffee.' He went inside the cook tent; it was vacant, but a fire in the sheet-iron stove kept the coffeepot warm. He poured for the three of them, then stood with his back resting lightly against the tent pole. 'Did you make a clean break, Betty?'

'As clean as one can make with my father.' She looked at Ben Holliday and could see that he wanted an explanation. 'Did you know that Jim and I once planned to get married?'

'I heard about that, yes.'

'We should have,' Betty Singer said. 'Only we didn't. Family loyalty got in the way. Father and Carl were grabbing land then. Carl lost his head and killed a man. I was there and saw it all. When Jim demanded the truth, what could I say? He was my own brother.'

'I forced the issue,' Jim Bender said. 'I demanded that she consider the truth of the thing and to hell with her family. I had no right

170

to ask that of you, Betty. It took me a year to get it through my head that I was asking her to put a rope around Carl's neck. It's better that he got away with it, Ben. Do you see that?'

'Yes, I see it,' Holliday said. 'People say a lot of things that are hard to take back.' He fell silent for a moment. 'But you'd better understand something, Miss Singer. I'll either have to get your brother, or someone else will. He killed Ollie Skinner.'

Jim Bender said, 'Don't pump her, Ben. If she knows anything, she keeps it to her self. It'll be bad enough, living after Carl gets what's coming to him, without having to know she tipped the scales against him.'

'All right,' Holliday said. 'I've got enough anyway. Nothing I could take to court, but I'm learning that out here you do with what you have.' He finished his coffee and got up. 'Jim, you watch out for her. Tomorrow, put her in the caboose and lock the doors.'

'Don't spend any time worrying about her,' Bender said softly.

After hesitating a moment, Holliday went out, thinking that this was a hell of a time for two people to get together. But then he supposed any time was good when you were in love. Colonel Dawson was by the locomotive, talking over the situation with Sergeant DuJoise; he turned to Holliday as he came up.

'DuJoise estimates that the total force may swell to a hundred and fifty. Which makes a knotty problem of it, Holliday.' He fingered his mustache. 'I've put Gary and a squad at the rear of the train. A little enfilade fire might turn an attack. At least the first wave.'

Jacques DuJoise made a wry face. 'With a force such as that, they could lose thirty men in the first attack and never miss them.'

'We can't stand to lose five,' Ben Holliday said. 'Did you take a nose count?'

'*Oui*. Forty-six, counting the cook, and the colonel's detail.' He gave his waxed mustache a twirl. 'Well, m'sieus, it might be more glorious to die outnumbered than the other way around.'

'I'm too old to die,' Cameron Dawson said, smiling. 'Just getting to the point where life is fun.' He slapped his lean stomach. 'We'll be smart to get some sleep. Breakfast ought to be an hour or so before dawn, Holliday. We'll all fight better on a full stomach.'

Holliday and DuJoise settled down in the cab of the engine, stretching out on the steel floor with only a blanket to soften it.

'It is sad to think of,' DuJoise said, 'but before this day, your plan for making peace held some hope; there was only the railroad for them to forget. But now, there's going to be dead brothers to forget. I'm afraid there won't be any peace, m'sieu.'

'A man can't have everything,' Ben Holliday said.

'Bender seems to have,' 'DuJoise said. He

172

turned his head and peered at Holliday. 'He's a wandering man these last few years. I know him well enough to say that. He loves the Singer woman. Maybe she loves him too, or she wouldn't have come here.'

'She didn't know he was here,' Holliday said.

'So? He was here.' He lay back, hands behind his head, then he suddenly reared erect, as did Holliday; they bumped their heads and cursed. Out on the flats, from the Indian camp, came the rattle of small-arms fire and the whooping surprise of many men.

One of the railroaders, startled from his sleep, panicked and yelled, *'Attack!'*

Instantly Jim Gary's shrill voice shouted, 'Quiet that man! Knock him out if you have to!'

The soldiers maintained order and Colonel Dawson came up; they stood there together and studied the fight taking place out there. It was too far to distinguish even the shadows of mounted men, but they could see the lances of bright muzzle flares as the fight grew hot, then dropped off to spasmodic shooting.

'What the hell caused that?' Dawson asked absently. 'If I didn't have better sense, I'd say a force rode through the Indian camp.'

'Riders coming!' A guard shouted this, then the sound of mounted men approaching grew louder. Holliday grabbed up his rifle and ordered a bright fire built up. The guards let

173

them through, eleven Texans; a few horses with empty saddles tagged along.

Murray Singer flung off and his face was gray in the firelight; he shook his head like a man struck numb. 'We lost twelve at least. Carl, for Christ's sake, find out how many. Vale? Where's Vale?' He looked around for the man and saw that he was gone. 'Dead? Jesus, I didn't think there was more than forty–fifty. A hundred anyway.' His attention focused on Ben Holliday and a smear of anger came into Murray's eyes. 'Your goddamned doing with the railroad.'

Holliday knew that Murray was going to jump him; it was simply a feeling he had, and when Singer swung toward him, Holliday brought the butt of the rifle up in an arc, laid it alongside Singer's jaw hinge, and dropped him instantly. Carl, hanging back, growled something, and John-Jack DuJoise pulled his pistol and cocked it.

'Dying is an easy thing, my friend.'

'What the hell's the matter with you people?' Dawson snapped. 'Don't you have better sense than to ride through an Indian camp?'

Bert Hutchins shifted his feet awkwardly and said, 'We used to hit 'em like that in the old days, Colonel. It worked then.'

'Sure, with a hundred Texans against thirty Comanches.' He waved his hand in disgust. 'Well, get settled for the night. They'll get even in the morning for this, and I hope you haven't lost all your fight.'

'Now just a damned minute—' Carl flared.

Dawson spun toward him, his manner threatening. 'Shut your mouth! I've just seen some Texas stupidity. Now don't tell me how tough you are; I already know how tough that is.' He pivoted on his heel and went back to his blankets. When Holliday turned, he saw Jim Gary there.

They walked back to the locomotive together. 'The old man's got his back up,' Gary said. He glanced at Holliday. 'I hope that if I get shot tomorrow, it'll be from the front. A man never really knows how he will do, does he?'

'You'll do all right,' Holliday said. 'Don't worry about it.'

'Well,' Gary said, 'It's nice that someone has confidence.' He walked back to his own place, and Holliday got into the locomotive. One of the railroad men DuJoise had picked stirred and said something about damn-fool Texas cowboys, and Holliday let it go, not wanting to talk about it.

He couldn't figure why Singer had showed up at all, but he soon got his answer when Carl Singer came up with Sergeant DuJoise.

'Where's my sister?' Carl asked flatly.

'With Bender,' Holliday said. 'Leave them alone.'

'She's going back with us,' Carl said.

175

'Why, because she knows too much?'

Singer laughed. 'Look Holliday, I don't want to argue about it. You just tell me where she is and we'll leave.'

'What, and miss the fun in the morning?'

'I'm not going to fight the damned Indians for the railroad,' Carl said. 'Pa already got too many men killed ridin' through that camp. I thought he had better sense.'

Holliday came to the ladder and stood there a moment. 'Carl, I don't think you're going to leave here. You want to know why? I'd already made up my mind to come after you for killing Skinner. You saved me the trouble by coming to me.'

For a moment Singer said nothing, then he laughed. 'What the hell are you talking about?'

'You killed Skinner.'

'Prove it.'

'I'm not going to try,' Ben Holliday said. 'I'm going to hang you on my own say-so. From what I've heard, it's long overdue.'

Singer laughed again, but it wasn't a laugh of pleasure. Hearing it, Ben pulled his weight up by his arms, arched his body, then came flying down, his knees striking Carl Singer squarely in the chest. The blow stunned him, and Holliday's weight carried the man to the ground. And when Holliday rolled away, Singer lay there, gagging for breath.

'Put a guard on him,' Holliday said, and DuJoise disarmed the man. 'I want him to survive, John-Jack. His neck will just fit a good rope.'

'M'sieu, let me turn him over to the colonel.'

'I'll take care of it myself,' Holliday said.

'You're making a mistake. Let the law do it. Not railroad law, but everyone's law.'

Holliday shook his head. 'There's no jury of Texans who'd convict him and you know it, and if you try a man once for the crime he can't be tried again.'

'A chance we all take. Bender waited, didn't he?'

'I'm not Bender. Now put a railroad man to guard him, and keep the Texans away from him.' He turned and mounted the cab again, knowing that DuJoise would do as he was told, whether he liked it or not.

Lying there, trying to get to sleep, Holliday understood fully that he was wrong, yet he felt helpless to change anything. He just had to hit out at the Singers and hurt them now; he felt that the death of the son would break the father, and he kept telling himself that it was for the railroad, but he knew it wasn't.

He just wanted to draw some blood of his own, right or wrong.

Jim Bender woke him and the air was very chilly; Holliday suspected that dawn was not far away.

'What's the matter, Jim?' He sat up and pawed sleep from his eyes.

'Got somethin' to tell you,' Bender said. 'You won't like it.'

'So tell me.'

'I turned Carl Singer loose.'

Holliday fisted a handful of the man's coat and tried to shake him. 'You what?''

'Told you you wouldn't like it,' Bender said. 'Ben, I wanted Carl once myself, and I still do. So go get him with a rifle or a six gun or a hand ax. But get him fair, Ben. You'll sleep better.'

CHAPTER TEN

With dawn so near, Ben Holliday forgot about sleep and left the locomotive cab; he walked over to where the cook was building a fire, and stood by it for a time to drive the chill from him. The soldiers were up and moving quietly about, and while Holliday stood by the fire, Lieutenant Gary walked over, his young face grave.

'Those Texans—ah—I took their guns away from them, Mr. Holliday. The old man is in a fit; I think he'd kill you on sight.'

'Let's go talk to him,' Ben Holliday said. 'Where are they?'

'Locked in the supply car,' Gary said. 'Hell, I didn't know what to do with them.'

He led the way, walking along the dark roadbed beside the train. The railroad men were stirring and walking around aimlessly with rifles and shotguns. Two soldiers from Gary's section guarded the supply car, and he motioned for them to open the door. Bert Hutchins stuck his head out and Murray Singer rudely pulled him back in. When he saw Ben Holliday he swore softly.

'I'm going to kill you. Carl!' He turned and gave his sleeping son a kick in the ribs. 'Get up, goddamit!'

'It's almost dawn,' Holliday said. 'If you

179

want to leave now, I'll give you the chance.' He stepped close to Murray Singer and took a handful of lapel. 'I don't need you here, and I don't want you here. You can get out if you travel west. When this is over, look for me. I'm going to clean house good.'

'You ride on me, Holliday, and you'll get yourself killed.' He jumped clumsily to the ground, then spoke to his friends. 'Come on, let's get the hell out of here. I never wanted to fight Indians for the railroad in the first place.'

Bert Hutchins got down and said, 'Since I'm here, I'll stay. You go to hell, Murray. I should have told you that years ago.'

'Don't get your back humped,' Singer said. 'A few years back when you were grabbing all the land you could get, I helped you, made you what you are today.'

'Sure, and I've kissed your ass ever since. What am I today, Murray? I don't have any friends except you and Vale, and he's dead. What am I going to tell his wife, Murray? His kids? That he died doing what Murray Singer wanted? I think they're getting a little tired of hearing that. My family is.'

'If you turn on me now, Bert, you've turned for good. No one gets a second chance.'

Bert Hutchins laughed softly. 'Hell, who wants a second chance to go on with you, Murray?'

Carl nudged his father. 'It looks like it's going to be light pretty soon. If we're goin'

180

then let's go. I want to be a few miles away before the sky turns pink.'

'All right,' Murray said. 'Where're our horses?'

'Get their horses,' Holliday said to Lieutenant Gary.

'Colonel Dawson isn't going to like this,' Gary said, then shrugged. 'Come on then. It's no skin off my nose.'

Four of Murray Singer's men remained still while the rest started to move away. Singer said, 'Well, what the hell's the matter with you?'

'This looks like a good time to quit,' one man said. 'We'll stay. Can't see any sense of going on with this.' He glanced at the others for approval, and found it.

Singer was angry and it made his voice raspy. 'All right, you yellow bastards. Any man who'd desert his brand is a yellow bastard.'

'It's getting light, Pa,' Carl said. 'You want to stand here and cuss 'em out, you go ahead. I'm leaving.' He swung his head around to face Ben Holliday. 'Where's Betty? She's coming back with us.' His voice was full of stubbornness, and Ben Holliday almost laughed at him for being so stupidly single-minded. But he didn't laugh. Instead he thought that here was a Singer weakness, an inability to give from a predetermined course, to change their minds once they'd made them up.

Holliday said, 'Get the hell out of here while the getting is good. This is your last chance.'

Carl was all for staying, arguing this out, but his father roughly shoved him into motion, and they followed Gary to where their horses were being held. A few minutes later they were mounted and leaving the camp, turning west where the prairie was void of Indians. It would mean a few extra miles skirting them, but well worth the trouble.

Around the cook tent, men clustered for their coffee and bacon, and Ben Holliday got a cup and filled it, then went back to the engine where DuJoise and Jim Bender sat.

'Sky is getting lighter,' said Bender.

The ink shadows were gradually rinsing away, and Holliday turned his attention to the Indian camp; considerable activity indicated that their painting and singing was done with. He said, 'John-Jack, how's this going to be? Will they come straight at us?'

'They are simple, and it's the only way they know of doing a thing.' He reached for his rifle, checked the action, then laid out a belt of cartridges. 'Watch the sky. At the first tinge of pink, they'll come.'

Colonel Dawson approached the locomotive cab and climbed partially up the ladder. 'I'm going to run my detail on the "horn," Holliday,' he said. 'The sound of a bugle has some effect on Indians. Mr. Gary has his section in place and will pay particular attention to guarding the caboose.' He blew out a long breath. 'I believe everything is ready. The waiting is hell though.'

He stepped to the ground and went back to his duties, and the end of track camp grew silent and watchful. As the dawn bloomed, visibility reached out onto the prairie, then the sky turned a pale rose and a deeper hush fell.

Holliday kept wondering what the first sensation would be when the Indians attacked, and when it came the drumming thunder of running ponies, he was relieved to find it not frightening at all. They came on in a clumsy drawn knot, blackening the prairie, shouting, waving their weapons, lashing their ponies to a frenzy of speed.

It was inevitable that some of the railroad men would start shooting too soon, when the range was too great, wasting precious ammunition, but it couldn't be helped, and Holliday didn't worry about it. He and Bender and DuJoise and the three others waited until the range was less than a hundred yards, then they fired on Colonel Dawson's bugle call, holding steady, squeezing off, and reloading.

The steel butt plate gave him a solid thump in the shoulder, and it felt good, almost pleasurable when he saw an Indian spin off his horse. The Indians hit the train in a milling jumble, wheeling and shooting, unable to change direction or organize themselves into a solid attacking force. The besieged fired down on them, scattered them, and sent them away to form again.

Fallen braves dotted the prairie, and Holliday thought that their numbers were miserably small. It was a strange thought for a man to have, he decided—regret that more of the enemy had not been killed. But this was war, in a small sense, and the winner would be determined by the number he could slay.

'Here we go!' Bender shouted as the Indians formed a line abreast and rode directly at the entire length of the train. They came on without pause, as though they intended to run right over them all, and they met a withering, determined fire before breaking into two lines, riding along the train until they came to the ends, there circling to attack the other side.

It was a heartbreaking maneuver, destined to fail because the train was too long, and as the Indians rode along, they came under the full fire of every man. A few railroad men died that time, but the Indians suffered a staggering loss.

When they pulled away, powder smoke hung heavily over the line of flatcars and John-Jack DuJoise roughly counted the dead. 'They can't stand much of this, m'sieu. Another wave, and if we hold, they are beaten.'

'It's almost too easy,' Holliday said without thinking, and both men looked at him.

Jim Bender grinned. 'You're getting some prairie sense, Ben. I was thinking that myself.'

The Indians retreated out of rifle range and drew together for a lengthy discussion. And after fifteen minutes of this, Ben Holliday decided that there wasn't going to be another attack. Not just yet.

'They're cooking up something,' Bender said. 'I don't like it.'

Colonel Dawson came trotting up; he pulled himself into the cab. 'Something's going on out there that I don't figure. They know now they can't push the train off the tracks, and we're well enough barricaded so they can't hope to kill us off in another attack. Mr. Holliday, it might be prudent if we backed this train out of here and left the field. I think there'll be enough death-song singing to convince them they didn't lick us.'

'Hey! Hey!' Bender said sharply, and pointed.

The Indians were spreading out into a huge circular line that threatened to surround the train. They took care to stay out of rifle range.

'I've never seen that maneuver before,' Dawson said, frowning.

Bender and John-Jack watched the Indians carefully, then the Frenchman swore. 'They're going to fire the prairie! Look at the grass, like tinder and there's no wind to speak of.'

'With all the creosote around here,' Holliday said, 'this train will burn like a candle.'

'There goes the first one,' Bender said,

pointing. Even as he spoke, the Indians were lighting their fires and fanning the small blazes to life with blankets. 'Backfire!' he said, and jumped down.

They seemed to accept Bender's authority without question, and Dawson and Holliday took charge of a section as a pall of smoke began to rise from the Indian fires.

They worked along both sides of the train, spading loose soil away from the train, then lighting their own fires. Blankets and slickers kept it away from the train and moving into an ever-widening circle, and the smoke choked them and made their eyes burn, and sparks burned holes in their clothes.

Holliday lost track of time, but finally the train rested in a blackened, smoking, patch of land, and they were safe, albeit exhausted and indescribably dirty. The fire was burning itself out, leaving a dirty patch of smoke to soil the blue morning sky, and the Indians rode around the circle, angry at being outdone but unable to do anything about it.

The fight was over and the railroad was still there for all purposes undamaged, and the Indians knew it. With a final wail of disappointment, they turned and rode away; Ben Holliday then started to assess the damage.

At the final tally, six men were dead and three more wounded, but not too seriously, and Holliday counted himself lucky. He supposed that as a gesture of defiance to the Indians, as a symbol of his victory over them, the camp should be restored as it was before, with a telegrapher and cook and work crew on duty. He gave Bender orders to see that this was done, then walked to the caboose and stepped inside.

Betty Singer was sitting on one of the hard benches combing the dirt out of her hair. Smoke still remained in the coach, and Holliday opened the other door to induce some air circulation.

'Your father and brother are gone,' he said.

'I don't care now.'

He shrugged. 'All right. What are you going to do now?'

'Go where Jim Bender goes,' she said. 'I've waited too long, Mr. Holliday.'

'It makes sense. I'm not going to ask you anything about your father or Carl. But I've got to tell you what I'm going to do.'

'You don't have to tell me,' she said softly. 'I know.'

He seemed relieved about it; he didn't relish the idea of telling her he was going to kill her brother. 'I'm not going to take Jim Bender with me,' Holliday said. 'I don't want anything to stand between you. Not anything like this. The railroad will break your father, but Jim Bender doesn't have to be part of it.'

'Thank you for that.' She stood up and tried to brush the soot from her dress but only

187

succeeded in smearing it. 'What makes a man want to own everything, Mr. Holliday?'

'I don't know. Can't you answer that? Don't you know your own father?'

'No, and I'm sure he doesn't know himself. He has to have things for no other reason than just wanting them.'

Holliday turned to the door. 'It's Carl I'm after, Betty. He killed Skinner.'

'Don't go after him alone,' she warned, then pressed her lips tightly together; it was the only advice she was going to give him. He waited a moment longer, then stepped down from the caboose and walked rapidly toward Colonel Dawson's position. He was being a fool, he told himself, but he *was* going to do this alone, without Bender or Sergeant DuJoise.

It was railroad business, strictly.

*   *   *

Adam Holliday stepped down from the coach at Dodge City, then turned to help his father with the suitcases. Julius Holliday wore a frown and a wrinkled suit and an air of impatience. He said, 'Check to see if there's a train south. It's too much to hope for, but check anyway. I'll sit in the shade.'

Adam carried the suitcases over to one of the benches, and Julius Holliday lowered his bulk with a sigh. He checked his watch against the depot agent's time while he waited, then

Adam came back.

'A freight is leaving in about a half hour,' he said. 'There's a coach on the tail end of it.'

'Damn it,' Julius said. 'Not even time for a man to get his supper.'

'Father, you ought to make up your mind,' Adam said. 'First you fuss because there won't be a train, and now you're—'

'Don't tell me what I'm doing,' Julius Holliday said. 'I was a fool to come along in the first place.'

'You insisted, Father.'

'Who can argue with a lawyer,' Julius said, then stood up. 'Let's go to the coach. It may be cooler there.' He hefted one of the suitcases. 'Wouldn't you think that it would cool off at sundown?' They walked along the siding, cinders crunching beneath their feet, and Julius spoke in a grumbling voice. 'Why the devil Ben couldn't meet us is beyond me.'

'You didn't wire that you were coming,' Adam said. 'I wanted to, but you said no.'

They found the train, loaded with army horses. The coach was next to the caboose, and when they drew near, Anna Neubauer and her father stepped away from the door so they could step up. Julius hauled himself to the platform, then turned to take the bags from his son. Anna Neubauer looked at Adam Holliday, then stepped forward and touched him on the arm.

'Why, you're Ben's brother, aren't you?'

'Yes,' Adam said, smiling. 'And hello, hello. Any friend of Ben's is a friend of mine. But he never told me about you.'

'He's been busy,' Anna said.

Adam nodded and continued to smile. 'And I don't blame him. Allow me to introduce my father, Mr. Julius Holliday, who either owns all the railroads, or is working on it. Miss, ah—'

'Anna Neubauer.' She introduced her father, who shook hands self-consciously.

Then Julius said, 'Can't we sit down?'

'I hope you're going south?' Adam said, taking Anna's arm to help her aboard.

'Oh, yes,' she said. 'We've been waiting for the train to get back.'

Julius, who was finding his seat, said, 'Where's it been?'

'To the end of the track,' Anna told him. 'Ben's there now. They're fighting the Indians.'

Julius stared for a moment, then shrugged it off as foolish talk. But Adam took it more seriously. 'Do you mean that? I can't believe it.' He sat beside her with the assurance that he would be welcome. 'Ben doesn't know anything about fighting Indians.'

'I think he's learning quickly,' she said, smiling at him. 'Don't you have any confidence in Ben?'

'It's not a matter of confidence,' Julius said flatly. 'You can't fight Indians and run a railroad too.'

Neubauer, who was lighting his pipe; looked

190

around and said, 'I tink he must fight first, or haf no railroad to run.'

'This convsation is going to have some exciting possibilities,' Adam said

The conductor came into the coach and walked toward them; he had a fare book in hand and Julius Holliday seemed insulted by it. 'I'm Julius Holliday, a board member of this line,' he said. 'Don't you have passes?'

'Can't pay the bills with passes,' the conductor said dryly. 'Mr. Holliday, ah, Ben, that is, did away with those the first week. That'll be four eight-five apiece.'

'Remind me to talk to Ben about this,' Julius said, and paid up. 'What a way to run a railroad! Conductor, do you know anything about the trouble at end of track?'

'Well, there were considerable Indians about,' he said. 'But I don't think they'll tear up the rails.' He touched a finger to the hard brim of his cap and moved on to the rear platform. A half dozen passengers wandered aboard, and the conductor took their money like a streetcar change maker.

Julius Holliday settled back in his seat and stripped the wrapper from a cigar. After he lit it, he said, 'I don't suppose you could tell me, miss, just what my son hopes to gain by fighting the Indians?'

'They believe the railroad is a bad thing,' Anna said. 'It frightens the buffalo.'

'Somewhere,' Julius said, 'there must be a

connection, but I fail to see it. Well, we'll get it all straightened out at the board meeting. Even if we have to elect a new chairman. Now, what's pleasant to talk about? I understand it's a long ride.'

*   *   *

Ben Holliday did not discuss his plans with Jim Bender or Sergeant DuJoise. Instead, he sent Bender along with the work train, and the Frenchman was left in charge of the end of track camp. The train pulled out for the main yard shortly after sundown, and the army left to make a wide four-day sweep to keep the Indians under constant eye. Holliday sat in the cook tent and waited for the camp to settle down for the night before leaving.

DuJoise would want to come with him, and Ben Holliday thought it best if he did not. There would be a stink over this, and there was no need to mix the army into it. Any man as big as Murray Singer had political friends who'd see that some sweating was done, and Ben wanted it to be a railroad affair.

There was no definite plan in his mind when he quietly saddled a horse and eased out of camp. He took a pistol with him and some spare shells, and a determination to finish a nasty job; anything else was just excess baggage. He'd been in the Singer house enough to know his way around it, and he

192

wasn't too worried about the hands in the bunkhouse. They'd be thinking about the dead friends they'd left on the prairie after that ride through the Indian camp, and Holliday didn't think any of them would take a side in this personal fight. There was no way of knowing how they felt about Satchel's killing, but four men had quit the brand, and he suspected that the whole thing sat poorly with them.

He had a long ride ahead of him, and he was tired and dirty and a long way from his Chicago-bred ideals. The thought that he could ride after a man to possibly kill him didn't alarm him as much as it amazed him; there was nothing in his background that offered a foundation for violence. He'd had a few fights in his life, but not over anything serious.

But he really couldn't see any alternative. There was no law to turn to, and if there was, what could he really say? That Carl Singer killed in cold blood? True or not, there was a matter of proof.

Well, he thought, there was one thing about Texas that had its good point. A man could settle his own trouble here, any way he saw fit, and if justice seemed to be served by it, people were willing to let it go at that.

If he settled this tonight, he'd have to go on, finish what he started, which was making the railroad pay. One way or another, peace would have to be made with the Indians; a man couldn't have them shooting up the coaches or setting fire to the prairie. And Murray Singer wouldn't be the only man who'd come along and try to saw the props out from under a tottering enterprise. You could spike the guns of one, but another always wheeled machinery into battery. Probably Holly Bristow would represent them too; he was a man who liked a fat commission.

Holliday thought a bit about the report he'd be writing to his father; that would make some reading. Be some howling over it too. But that was somewhere tomorrow and this was tonight, and the two bits of business were a long way apart.

The Singer place was dark when he arrived. He dismounted some distance from the house and hunkered down to look things over. He couldn't quite make up his mind as to whether the dark house was a natural state, or whether it was dark for other reasons. As he recalled, there was always a light on somewhere, but he couldn't be sure.

Carefully he approached the bunkhouse and circled it twice before stopping at the door. A heavy wrought-iron hasp hung on its hinge, and he moved on to the tool shed and there found a spike. With this securely wedged into the loop passing through the hasp, he felt sure that they weren't going to boil out of there shooting. Of course they could break out the windows, but he'd hear that and be warned by it.

Holliday returned to the house and stayed close to the walls, moving quietly and slowly all the way around it. The back door was locked and so were the windows, and he tried them all, finding only the one on the side porch open.

He didn't go inside immediately, but thought about this a bit. It struck him as strange that all the doors would be locked except one. And all the windows too. He could understand the doors, but not the windows for the night was warm and windows were opened to cool a house.

The suspicion that he was being invited to use one door only firmed up in his mind, and he became cautious. Quite likely either Carl or his father had taken him very seriously and had something waiting for him in the nature of a fatal surprise. Now what would it be? Was Carl sitting in that darkened room waiting for the door to be opened?

Holliday didn't think so. Carl might have to sit up too many nights, and it just wasn't his way of doing a thing. The man had a sneaky mind, so Ben suspected that Carl had rigged up something else, something to do the job while he slept.

It would have to be simple, something in the line of a snare; Carl wasn't very original in his thinking, so Holliday mulled this over for a few minutes. A gun was probably set to go off as soon as the door opened; Holliday assumed it was a gun because Carl was familiar with them, more so than with other weapons.

A shotgun quite possibly, for a single bullet from a pistol or rifle might miss. A double charge of buckshot would do nicely, Ben thought, and went on that assumption.

He considered the possibility that Carl had wired the door knob, but discarded that for two reasons: the setup would be overly complicated, and the charge would have to pass through the door to get the man.

No, it would go off after the door opened. Probably a string or a stick trigger that would release when the door opened enough to admit a man.

Leaving the porch, Holliday rummaged around the corral until he found a stick at least eight feet long. He took this back with him and, crouching down to one side, reached up and turned the knob. The stick eased the door open, way open, until it bumped gently against the back wall, and there was no blast, no string attached.

Unwilling to abandon his theory. Holliday turned this over in his mind and decided that there was a string stretched across the room, something for a man to tangle his feet in, and he laid down, belly flat, and poked into the room with the long stick. He couldn't hope to set off the snare by contacting the wire with the butt end, so he raised the stick up gently until he contacted something. Then he gave it a tug, and a double-barreled shotgun roared and sprayed shot a few feet over his head.

Yelling like a man cut in half. Holliday jumped up and ducked into the darkened room. From another part of the house, he heard a pair of boots hit the floor; Carl had obviously been waiting in bed. From somewhere else, a door slammed, and Murray Singer yelled, 'You got him, boy!'

Holliday plucked the pistol from his belt and cocked it and stood there, holding it in his hand. It was an odd feeling to hear Singer yell like that, use those words, for if he were really dead, that was all Singer would think of it. He'd be elated and not a damned bit sorry.

A smear of lamplight started down the far hall and Holliday watched it grow in brightness, then Carl burst into the room, playing the light on the floor where he expected the body to be. He looked expectant—and surprised and disappointed when he saw nothing.

Then Ben spoke. 'Over here, Carl.'

Singer threw the lamp and whipped up his pistol just as Ben Holliday shot. He heard Carl grunt as the bullet found a home, then there was a slithering as he fell to the floor.

The burst lamp spread coal oil over the rug, and the flames caught instantly, leaping to great brightness. Holliday could see Carl Singer, a well of blood in the middle of his chest, and eyes already growing dead.

He didn't stay. Ducking out; he was already dashing around the house when he heard Murray Singer's anguished shout. Holliday ran for his horse, then stopped and ran back to the bunkhouse. The hands were driving their shoulders against the door, trying to get out, and with the barrel of his pistol he broke away the spike, freeing them.

They seemed to explode from the door, some falling down in their hurry. They saw him, but ignored him, and ran toward the house, which was now hopelessly afire.

No one noticed Ben Holliday leave.

CHAPTER ELEVEN

Sergeant Jacques DuJoise was up and about when the cook lit his breakfast fire, and he took the first cup of coffee from the pot. He stood outside the tent and watched the dark sky give way to the dawn flush. His sleep had been troubled since he had discovered that Ben Holliday had gone without him, and DuJoise's first impulse had been to catch up a horse and follow him. Then he thought about it and stayed in camp, for a man's business was his own; Holliday obviously had wanted it that way for he had gone to a lot of trouble to see that Jim Bender had gone back to Comanche and that DuJoise had remained in camp.

Still this logic didn't keep the Frenchman from worrying. He liked Ben Holliday, liked the man's straight-out approach to his problems, liked the way he thought things out, without a lot of mental muss and clutter and no deep regrets afterward. It would be a pity, DuJoise thought, if some wild Texan like Carl Singer did him in; the future held something for men like Holliday.

He finished his coffee and let the cup dangle from the hook of his finger, unable to give up his vigil. The sky turned rose, then a sliver of molten sun shot brightness across the flats, and he saw the lone horseman approaching, far out, coming slowly, in no particular hurry. DuJoise stared a moment, identified Ben Holliday, then laughed with relief and went inside for another cup of coffee and his breakfast.

DuJoise was finishing his meal when Holliday stopped outside and dismounted. He came in, his step weary, and went directly to the coffeepot. Lack of sleep cast harsh lines into his face and made his shoulders round. DuJoise said, 'I know it's done or you wouldn't be back.'

'It's done,' Holliday said, sitting down. 'More than I figured. Carl threw the lamp just before I shot him. The place was going up in smoke when I left.' He folded his hands around the coffee cup. 'So it's either over with Murray Singer, or just beginning. He's got enough influence to bring legal action.'

'Doesn't the railroad have any lawyers?'

'Lawyers cost money, especially railroad lawyers.' He sighed and sagged forward, his forearms flat on the table. 'But that's something I'm not going to worry about now, John-Jack. I don't want this Indian business hanging where it is, with blood spilled. We've got to try again for peace.'

'*Oui*, it's a good thing. But how can you bring about a meeting?'

Holliday shrugged. 'Lieutenant Gary's pretty original. Why don't you ride to Elliot and talk it over with Colonel Dawson? If you come up with an idea, let me know. I'm going back to Comanche.'

'We can try,' DuJoise said. 'I'll leave for the post right away. When are you going north?'

'When I wake up,' Holliday said. 'I may sleep for a week.'

He went out and walked a few yards away to one of the maintenance supply tents and made a bed for himself on some sugar sacks. The camp was turning noisy now as the railroad men went into the cook tent for breakfast, but this didn't bother him; he fell asleep and didn't wake up until late that night.

Without waking the cook, Holliday put some cold meat and a half loaf of bread in a sack, filled his canteen, then put the handcar onto the tracks and began to pump himself north. He was in no particular hurry, but kept steadily at it until dawn, then wrestled the car off the tracks and slept in the shade of it. At dusk he woke, ate cold meat and bread, then began to pump away the last miles of his journey.

When he reached the yard, he put the car away and walked to the headquarters building. It was dark except for a lamp in the bottom hall. Making his way up the stairs, he opened the door to his room and crossed immediately to the bed. The moment he sat on it, he knew someone was in it, and when the man pawed out for him, Holliday balled his fist and hit where the jaw ought to be. He connected

201

solidly and the man shouted, half in anger and half in pain. Then he scrambled out of bed and lit the lamp, swearing all the while.

'This is a goddamned intrusion!' Adam Holliday said, then looked around to see who he was talking to. 'Ben! Well, for gosh sakes, Ben!'

'What the hell are you doing in my bed?' Ben asked.

'Sleeping, until you hit me in the face.' He rubbed the welt on his cheekbone. 'You're getting violent as hell. Father's here. In the hotel in town. And I met your blonde. Some dish.' He got up and pulled on his pants. 'You don't seem too happy to see me, Ben.'

'I'm glad to see you and you know it,' Ben said. 'But I didn't expect Father. Truthfully, I'd be a lot happier if he was in Chicago.' He went over the night stand, filled the washbowl, and scrubbed. 'I suppose he's ranting as usual?'

'Well, it's Father's only way of speaking,' Adam said. 'You get used to it. He's very impatient to see you.'

'You buy that stock like I asked you to?'

'Yes. And what a row that caused. If you want a reason for Father being here, blame it on that. You see, I'd just received a check from the Cartwright estate—a very handsome one, so I loaned you eight thousand. And I borrowed another six thousand from our dear, conservative brother. He thought I was buying some lake-shore frontage with it.' Adam rolled

202

his eyes toward the ceiling. 'So when Father read the market report and saw the flurry, he hit the ceiling. Well, the upshot is that Father considers me a fool and you a madman for not accepting that offer.'

'It wasn't legitimate,' Ben Holliday said. 'Besides, there is no more offer.'

'Oh? It's been withdrawn?'

'Definitely. I shot him the night before last.' Ben knew that Adam would be shocked, and it pleased him; he wanted Adam to know that he'd changed. Maybe Adam would communicate that to Julius Holliday, prepare him in a way for the rough sailing ahead.

'You mean, it was an accident,' Adam said.

'No, I mean that I took a gun and went after him, and when I found him I shot him before he shot me.' He dried himself and took off his shirt, then threw it in the corner. 'When it comes right down to it, a lawsuit can't hold a candle to a bullet for getting the job done.'

'Good grief! Is the law after you?'

'No,' Ben said. He shaved, using cold water and much stropping of the razor. 'Did you happen to meet Jim Bender? I want to find him.'

Adam Holliday frowned pleasantly. 'A tall, thin man? I think I saw him at the hotel. He had a woman with him.' He reached out and took Ben's arm. 'Don't you think you ought to sleep, or wait until morning?'

'Dirty jobs,' Ben said, 'I like to do now. No,

he's a railroad man. I only shoot the ones who aren't.' He reached out and pushed Adam flat in bed and threw the covers over his head, then went down the back stairs. The town was quiet when he walked toward it, well past the general closing hour, even for the saloon. The clerk was sleeping when Holliday entered the lobby, and rather than wake the man, Ben had his look at the register, saw which room Bender had, and went on up.

He knocked twice and got no response, then the door opened a crack and Bender thrust the muzzle of his pistol against Holliday's stomach.

'You're a cautious man,' Holliday said, and stepped inside.

Bender lit the lamp and put the gun away. 'I ought to have shot anyway. What the hell's the idea of leaving me behind? Did you think I'd draw the line because of Betty?'

'You've got enough troubles,' Ben said. 'I've got to tell Betty how it is now.'

'Just how is it now?' Bender asked.

'Carl's dead. He wired a shotgun trap for me, but I smelled it first. The place is burned to the ground.'

Bender whistled softly. 'Man, you really went Injun, didn't you?'

'The fire was an accident,' Ben said. 'Carl threw the lamp at me before the shooting started. The place caught afire. I'm going to have to tell Betty.'

'Just say that it's over,' Bender said. 'She knows already how bad it is.' Holliday frowned briefly and Bender explained. 'Ben, she knows what Carl deserves. Let it go at that.'

'All right,' Holliday said 'I sent DuJoise to the post to see if Dawson couldn't get the Indians together for a talk.'

Bender shrugged. 'Slim chance, but worth a try. What can you lose?'

'That's what I figured. I'm still determined to use the original plan, with the hot wires.' He toed a chair around and sat down. 'For the first time, I really think I can save this railroad, build it into something. For a fact, I worried more about Singer's attempt to buy it up than I did the Indians. Singer's kind of business is hard to fight. I'm glad it's off my back.'

'Someone else will come along, just as greedy as Singer.'

'Sure, but maybe I'll be in a better financial position to fight them.' He slapped his knees and stood up. 'I think I'll go root the old man out of bed; he hasn't seen the sun come up in thirty years.'

Bender stared at him for a minute, then laughed. 'Kind of like the mouse that got into the whisky bottle?'

'How's that?'

'He went out looking for cats to kick.'

'Well, something like that,' Ben Holliday said. 'Look, I know my father. He didn't come here for some grouse hunting.' Holliday put

205

the chair back against the wall and turned to the door. 'Of course I've got an advantage with my father that I never had with Singer: I know my father and what he'll say.'

'Knowing that much about some men has caused me to pack up and leave for healthier country,' Bender said. 'But go ahead. I admire a free-swingin' man.'

Returning to the lower floor, Holliday decided that if this whole thing went up in smoke, he wouldn't go back to Chicago at all, but team up with Jim Bender; he really liked the man, liked the way he thought about things; they could find some business venture, and not railroading.

Ben knew that his father would be in the best room available, so he walked along the hall to the back suite and knocked on the door. He had to ball his fist and pound several times before he got an answer, and that was a grumble.

'What do you want? And who are you?'

'It's Ben. Open the door.'

This did not erase Julius Holliday's irritation. He flung the door open and motioned the young man in. 'You damn fool, it isn't even daylight outside.' He fumbled around for the lamp, lit it, then sat heavily on the edge of the bed and pawed the sleep from his eyes. 'What possible reason could you have for this outrageous intrusion? Ooooo, what an unearthly hour for a man to rise.' He held his head in his hands for a moment, then looked at his son. 'I think you've lost your mind.'

'Adam thought so too,' Ben said. He went over to the windows and raised the curtains, letting them flap on the rollers. 'What did you come out here for, Dad?'

'Well, I wasn't getting proper action from you, Ben.'

Ben turned and looked at him. 'What did you want?'

'I wanted you to listen to me!' Julius snapped. 'That's what I wanted!' He calmed himself. 'Lovell wired me that you'd fired him. I made up my mind to come then.'

'I'd rather have you do your own snooping than hire it done,' Ben said. 'If you didn't fully trust me, then why give me the job?' He knew he wouldn't get an answer to that, and didn't wait for one. 'You sent me here to make the line pay, then recommended that I take Singer's offer. Why? So it would look good? So it wouldn't be put down as a failure for Julius Holliday?' Ben laughed softly. 'Well, if you want to sell it now, you'll have to rustle up another buyer. The three men that made the offer aren't interested now. Jerry Vale is dead. Bert Hutchins has backed out, and Murray Singer's been burned out, clean to the ground. And the price has gone up. Or don't you watch the markets?'

'I saw that flurry,' Julius snapped. 'Ben, that was the cheapest bit of conniving I ever saw. I suppose you wanted the stock up a half or so, then you'll dump yours and pocket the profit.'

The impulse to hit him was strong; he had never known it so strong before. But he resisted it. 'I want working capital. Not one share of my stock is for sale.'

Julius Holliday was surprised. 'What's that?'

Ben walked over and stood near his father, looking down at him, and it was an odd sensation; he had never known it before. 'I don't want to sell the line at any price, Dad. I want to stay with it, rise with it if it succeeds, and fall if it fails. All my life I've wanted to go it on my own. That's the way it's going to be this time.'

'I've only tried to help you,' Julius said.

'Sure, but I don't want any more help, Dad.' He pulled a chair around and sat down, facing his father. A gray light was seeping into the room; it would be dawn in another ten minutes. 'I don't want any advice, or money, or anything. This is going to be straightened out my way, or balled up hopelessly through my efforts. Either way, I'm going to learn my own lessons. Getting money is always going to be a problem, I'm afraid, so I might as well get used to the idea of it. The Indians—well, I hope that the railroad can make peace with them. At least that's one of my top priority projects for the near future. Maybe I'll succeed and maybe I'll fail. But I'll try, you see.'

'You're turning into a man, Ben,' Julius said.

'I like you better. And I'm sorry if I held you back.'

'Don't be sorry. It's a lesson I've learned in Texas: never be sorry. Good or bad, do what has to be done and don't cry about it.' He sighed and got up and walked back to the window and watched the sky turn rose. 'I don't know as you understand me, Dad. I don't really understand you. But why don't you go on back to Chicago and let me be? Not because I want to get rid of you. But because I want to be on my own. Will you do that for me?'

'It won't be easy. I'm full of advice. You know that.'

'Yes, but I'll get along without it.'

Julius Holliday chuckled. 'I met the German girl. Serious with you?'

'It might be in time,' Ben said. 'You'll like her; she isn't afraid of you at all.'

'I sure found that out,' Julius said. 'Ben, I'd like nothing better than to see you make it. Would you take my word that I won't interfere and let me stay a week or so? Just as a favor?'

'Sure,' Ben said, turning, a smile on his face. 'Why not?' He walked over to the chair that held his father's clothes, and tossed them to him. 'Come on, I'll buy you a Texas breakfast.'

*　　*　　*

It was a good feeling, Ben decided later, to get

209

the railroad on a schedule. It was good for business, too, for the freight manifests grew steadily fatter, and the revenue came in slowly but in steadily increasing amounts. In one week Midland-Pacific fulfilled an army contract and shipped Bert Hutchins' cattle. Vale's widow and half-grown son came to see Holliday; he was sorry the man was dead but didn't show any false grief, since the man had picked his side and lost.

She was selling out, and he gave her a good freight rate, then sent the train north with the largest single shipment so far. It created a stir in Dodge and in the Chicago market. Midland-Pacific stock took a substantial gain, and even shrewd investors began to consider it with something else besides disdain.

Yet Ben knew that the line was a long time away from being on firm financial footing, and he hoped he could keep the boat from rocking. Western Union cleaned out the telegraph equipment and sent in their own operators, and the line to Fort Elliot was finally finished. Some hailed this as a major communications advance, but Julius Holliday thought it was a bit of financial foolishness; the day would come when the railroad would regret parting with communication control.

On Thursday afternoon, Jim Bender brought Holliday the news that Murray Singer had ridden into town with six men, and that Singer wanted to see him at the hotel. Holliday took his .44 pistol from the drawer, made sure it was loaded, and thrust it into his waistband.

Then he walked uptown to find out what Singer had to say.

CHAPTER TWELVE

As Ben Holliday walked down the street, he wondered if the men with Murray were all he had left, and if they were, it was a pitiful number, considering the number Singer had once employed. Holliday could see that nearly everyone in town was gathered; if there was trouble, they wanted a front-row seat.

Approaching the hotel, Holliday didn't think about the odds; he knew how strong was Murray Singer's pride; this would be between the two of them, either talk or a fight. Singer and his men were arrayed across the front of the porch, and as Holliday stopped in the street, Jim Bender came out of the hotel and stood just behind the Singer faction.

Bender said, 'No need to turn around, gents. But just keep it in mind that I'm behind you. You go right ahead, Murray. Mr. Holliday's waitin'.'

Julius Holliday and Adam wheeled down the street in a buggy and pulled in by the feed store; neither man got down, but Julius said, 'Ben, this damned thing has gone far enough.' He started to dismount, but Murray Singer pointed a finger at him.

'If you're not carrying a gun, don't get down!' He turned his head slightly to speak to Jim Bender. 'My men will stay out of this. You don't have to interfere.'

'If they stay out,' Bender said, 'I won't interfere.'

Ben Holliday said 'What do you want to talk about, Murray?'

'Us,' Singer said softly, 'You killed my son and burned me to the ground. Did you think for a minute I'd let you get away with it?'

'I had hoped you had sense enough to,' Holliday said. 'Murray, ask yourself who's to blame. Who killed Skinner? Who set himself up against the railroad?'

'That part don't matter,' Murray said. 'I'm going to kill you just because I'll take pleasure in it.'

'Are you going to start shooting, Murray?'

'Hell, yes,' Murray said, and flipped his hand beneath his coat for his gun. He was slow by some standards, but compared to Holliday's inexperience he was very fast.

Holliday jerked at his pistol in his hurry to get it into action, and the hammer snagged on his shirt, ripping it, slowing him so much that Murray Singer had his first shot off before Ben was even ready to cock his gun. The bullet spun Ben around completely, and caused Murray to miss his second shot. Ben fell down but did not drop the .44. He brought it up, sighted, and shot Murray Singer high in the breastbone. Murray staggered back a step, hooked his heel against a crack in the porch planks, and went down hard. He kicked his legs and tried to rise, but the strength was leaving him and he died amid a fit of bloody coughing.

Julius and Adam left the buggy in a rush, and Singer's men just stood there as though they couldn't believe it had turned out this way. Jim Bender stayed behind them while a crowd gathered around Ben Holliday.

Julius was shouting, 'Someone get the doctor!'

Some wag standing by said, 'Hell, mister, he was on his way the minute he heard the first shot. Like a damned bird dog.'

'Ben, are you badly hurt?' This was Adam's concern; he raised Ben to a sitting position and looked at the blood on his coat, his manner horrified.

The doctor arrived, brusquely pushing people aside. He made a brief examination of the wound and said, 'I'll have to dig that out.' He stood up and motioned for Ben to be lifted. 'Cart him over to my office.'

'Gently there!' Julius snapped as two men grabbed Ben's feet. 'By God, I've never seen such people!'

The man lifting Ben's shoulders took offense at Julius' tone. 'You his mother or somethin'? Get the hell out of the way.'

Julius Holliday was infuriated because the doctor wouldn't allow him to be present when the bullet was removed, and it was an hour later before he and Adam were permitted to pull up chairs at Ben's bedside.

The young man's face was gray and he was in pain, but it didn't seem to bother him much. He looked at his father and said, 'Don't fuss around so much, Dad. You look like you've been sick.'

'I'm thinking of the lawsuit you're going to have.'

Ben shook his head. 'No, it's settled now. For good.' Someone knocked and Adam got up to open the door.

Jim Bender came in and grinned. 'You were slow as hell, Ben, but you got the job done. Which is what counts.' He sighed and sat down. 'Got to give Murray credit though; he went all the way.' His glance touched Julius Holliday. 'I don't expect you understand that.'

'Frankly, I don't.'

'Well,' Bender said, 'Murray wanted your railroad. And he went after it the only way he knew how. If he'd been like you, Mr. Holliday, he'd have tried some clever stock swindle or maneuver. But he wasn't a complicated man. He was just a hog who wanted it all and he grabbed and hung on and kicked until the other fella let go. Only Ben wouldn't let go, so Murray had to start shootin'.'

'You make it surprisingly clear,' Julius Holliday said softly. 'I was going to stay here a week or so until a few of these matters pending were settled. I think now that I'll go back to Chicago. Adam, you ought to stay and

215

help Ben until he gets on his feet. And I don't think you ought to stay here, Ben. Perhaps if I spoke to that German girl—It seems to me that she'd gladly—'

'Dad,' Ben said, 'will you stop running things for me?'

Julius Holliday laughed and seemed embarrassed; he got up and turned to the door. 'You're right, Ben. It's time I got out and let you handle your own business.'

He stepped out and closed the door softly. Jim Bender rolled a smoke and said, 'He's all right. Well, Betty's going to be needing me. In a couple days we ought to do something about the Indians, huh, Ben? A man's troubles never end but what something else comes up. I wonder what it'll be after the Indians?'

'I won't worry about it,' Ben Holliday said. He shifted, searching for a comfortable spot. 'This is the worst bed I've ever slept in.'

Jim and Adam went out and he was relieved to be alone. His wound pained him like blazes, but he could tolerate that. In his mind still was the memory of that moment when Murray Singer drew his gun; the thought had been strong then that he stood a good chance of dying, and the amazing part of it was that he had entertained no regrets at all; within him there was no apology for what he was or what he had done.

I'm going to be all right, Ben thought, then fell into a deep resting sleep.

We hope you have enjoyed this Large Print book. Other Chivers Press or G.K. Hall & Co. Large Print books are available at your library or directly from the publishers.

For more information about current and forthcoming titles, please call or write, without obligation, to:

Chivers Press Limited
Windsor Bridge Road
Bath BA2 3AX
England
Tel. (01225) 335336

OR

G.K. Hall & Co.
P.O. Box 159
Thorndike, Maine 04986
USA
Tel. (800) 223-2336

All our Large Print titles are designed for easy reading, and all our books are made to last.